TINAN HINAN

Copyright © A.E. Stewart 2016

Published by A.E. Stewart

Cover artwork by Gary Taaffe, Copyright © A.E. Stewart 2016
Formatting by Gary Taaffe, Copyright © A.E. Stewart 2016

ISBN: 978-0-9946151-5-2

Gary Taaffe
BunyaPublishing.com
BunyaPublishing@gmail.com

Book 4

TINAN HINAN

A.E. STEWART

Tinan Hinan

Africa 300-325 C.E. (Or 300 A.D.)

She was found in a basket made from bulrushes, floating on the River Nile. Many unwanted babies were disposed of this way. They were given an even chance of life. If the crocodiles didn't find them, perhaps some other childless couple would. This baby was blessed because she was delivered into the hands of a woman washing her laundry at the river's edge. When she was five years of age, her parents realised that this child was going to be special. She was bright and lively, taller than most other children of her own age, with the most beautiful pale blue eyes. It wasn't very long before the child was noticed by the priests at the temple where her mother worked. They encouraged her to learn the many different musical instruments as well as to sing to her own accompaniment. She was allowed to attend reading and writing classes with the other children of the Roman hierarchy. As she grew taller, showing great aptitude in learning and music, she was groomed by the priests to become a priestess.

The only problem was that she was haughty and often in trouble because of her inability to conform to discipline. Her best friend was an older girl called Takamat who suffered from a slight limp and stunted growth. Despite suffering from a disability, she had a bright intelligence to which Tinan was drawn, and they soon became inseparable.

When she reached puberty with a fast ripening body, Tinan showed such promise that her parents believed that she was destined for something more than a temple priestess. Even Pharaoh's wife was jealous as she watched her husband's interest grow when his eyes fell on Tinan. There was only one thing to do. That was to sell her and her crippled friend to a slave trader who would take her far away from Egypt. The order had been given. The next time that the girls were singing in the temple, they were pointed out by a priest to two Roman guards who had orders to remove the girls after their performance. Unfortunately one of them became besotted with Tinan's beauty and as he listened to her singing, forgot the reason for being there. She accompanied herself on the harp and her pure voice echoed from the walls of the temple, whilst Takamat sang harmony as she used small clappers or castanets. Dressed in an almost transparent white dress with her dark hair braided and beaded Tinan was truly regal. It would be easy to mistake her for a person of royal lineage.

Before they had time to realize what was happening both girls were roughly seized and marched outside into the waiting arms of two bearded ruffians. The Roman guard who had fallen under the spell of these two young girls was not happy about this outcome. He grumbled to his companion.

'This seems a little harsh. To sell these two into slavery at such a young age is not a usual practice. To tell you the truth I cannot understand why anyone would want to banish such a talented and beautiful child.'

'Marcus, don't worry about it. We have no say in what goes on at the Palace. We're just ordinary soldiers following orders, so forget about it.' As they had been gagged and bound, Tinan couldn't say a word but the look of defiance in her mesmerizing eyes would haunt Marcus for a long time.

The girls were taken to an older part of the town where they were roughly thrown into a room which had been used to store hay for cattle fodder. Before long a man entered. He was the slave trader who had been well paid to take these two as far away as possible.

'Well,' Ben leered. Let's have a look at what I've got: Nothing much, just a couple of small fish. If I haven't been paid by someone who wouldn't take no for an answer I would have thrown you back, but I suppose females are always saleable.'

On hearing these words, Tinan knew that her life had changed forever. She had heard stories about slave traders and the terrible fate which would await her at the hands of this man. Her innocence was about to disappear. She was kept in ankle chains attached to a pole in this awful smelly place. To relieve herself she had to drag the chains to a far corner and squat down on the hay. Takamat was not chained as she was made to carry the miserable meals to her friend, but both knew that escape was impossible. The two men who guarded them day and night were always outside. If anything, they seemed worse than their employer always leering with suggestive comments. After about a week Ben came in and informed them that they would be moving out in the morning. Neither girl had a change of clothing or any other toiletries. The fact that they both were dirty and miserable didn't worry their captor at all. They were pushed into a horse drawn cage, the gate was locked and they were prisoners again. There were two other girls sitting in this carriage. Tinan spoke to the older girl.

'Where are we going?'

'To the slave markets of course. Where do you think?' When she heard this, the smaller fair haired girl began to whimper but her companion just laughed.

'There is no point in taking that attitude. By this time tomorrow you will be a slave to someone who will own you forever.' More crying erupted until one of Ben's men came and hit the bars of the cage with a wooden club telling them to shut up.

Takamat whispered to the older girl.

'Will they sell us in this state? We are filthy. Who would want to buy someone in this condition?'

'Where have you been living? They don't care what we look like. We are only females to be owned by men and used as they see fit. Our condition is not important. We are only valued as another animal.'

That night they pulled into a market town where they slept in the carriage, but they were allowed out one at a time to urinate under the watchful eye of a guard. The morning came and the carriage was pulled over to the market place. Ben prodded the four girls, pointing to a cleared space in front of a group of noisy men who were pushing and shoving to get a better view. Tinan watched in horror as other females and a few males were pushed forward to be sold to the highest bidder. She turned to Takamat.

'Whatever you do, please take my hand and stand beside me. Perhaps we can be bought together by someone. I don't want them to split us up.' Ben pushed Tinan who grabbed her friend's hand so that they stood side by side. A voice from the crowd yelled out.

'They look a little young! What are they like under those rags?' Tinan gasped loudly as Ben ripped her robe from her body, leaving her standing there in her brief tanga. Her hands instinctively covered her breasts as the crowd laughed and called out insults. She bit her lip refusing to cry. Her shame and anger was well contained but she learned a lesson as to her place in the lives of men with power.

One particularly large and heavy man stepped forward with his bid. He wore the flowing robes of a nomad. He was the only bidder so he now owned her. She had taken Takamat's hand again and wouldn't let go of it. For some reason Ben took pity on Takamat, and said to the buyer.

'You can have this one too thrown in for the same price.'

The man agreed. Once again the two girls were enclosed in a cage and it was hauled away to the outskirts of town. He stopped here and ordered them out, telling his male slave.

'I want you to wash these two with water from that well then give them these clean clothes to put on. They stink. I will not take them anywhere with me in that state.' Takamat was fifteen years old, whilst Tinan was just thirteen. They grew up that day and learned a lesson which was never forgotten. Their new owner was not unkind, but Tinan knew by his glances that he was biding his time for something, and she instinctively knew that it was not pleasant. He was a Bedouin living and traveling across the desert, so he gave the girls to the other women who were to instruct them in the servile positions in his household. Sometimes they would ride the camels with the other women, while at other times Tinan would walk alongside the procession with the ships of the desert.

Omar's richly prized horses were not used by the women. Time seemed to be irrelevant but nearly two years had passed when their owner took his group to a pre-arranged meeting place where members of his tribe gathered for social activities. Tinan noticed a rock-pool there and was so keen to bathe that she forgot about asking permission. She wasn't aware that Omar had followed her, as he hid his presence by standing behind a rocky outcrop. Removing her clothes, she stepped into the luxury of cool water, feeling totally invigorated by the feel of the water all over her body. She ducked her head beneath the water and then rose with it running from her long black hair and down her body in glistening rivulets. As she waded out to pick up her clothes, Omar couldn't contain his lust.

'She is a goddess,' he thought to himself. ' One day I will have her.'

Many tents were erected that day. The men separated themselves into a group singing and dancing outside the tent, while the women gathered inside. Tea and coffee was served all night around the fire with goats and sheep sacrificed to feed the large hungry group. Takamat took her friend aside and suggested that they both should sing some of the songs which they had learned back in Egypt. As it was common practice to use castanets and drums they could improvise with hand clapping. Tinan agreed happily to involve the other women in the tent. Before too long they all began to clap in rhythm to the lovely erotic love song that the two girls were singing. The flap of the tent was lifted as two men entered to see who was responsible for the beautiful music. One was the master and the other was a younger man who couldn't take his eyes off Tinan. There are unspoken laws of the desert. It is very important to always show hospitality to guests so arguments rarely occur unless an insult or worse is given. Tonight her master was approached by the young man who wanted Tinan for his wife. Omar felt angry because he had plans for her that did not include giving her to this man, but he had no reason to refuse this honourable offer.

'She has no dowry. She is only a slave girl who is not worthy of you. There are other women here who would be more suitable. Don't be so hasty, sleep on it and tomorrow you will feel differently.' Omar didn't want to surrender this lovely young woman. He knew that she must be a virgin but he would have to find a more appropriate time and place for his possession of her. The next morning Omar found the young man at his tent again with the same request. This became difficult and by now the other members of his tribe knew about the situation. Omar had no more reasons to use to dissuade this would be suitor but he did have an idea.

'Although I cannot say that this woman is my kin, she has lived with me for a few years and has become one of the family. So if you are still resolute on your course to wed her I will allow this if you accept my challenge: A horse race.'

The young man heartily agreed because he believed that his horse was the swiftest and he knew that he carried less weight than Omar. Space was cleared around a track where the two men lined up. Great interest was shown by all gathered there. This was an exciting sporting challenge because it was said that these men loved their horses more than they loved their women. Tinan whispered to Takamat that this would be an ideal time to escape, but she knew that even if they managed to steal a horse or a camel, they would die of thirst out in the desert. They had no idea where they were anyway.

'Just be patient Tinan. The time will come for us to have our freedom. Perhaps we had better join the others and watch this event.'

Omar wasn't the leader of this caravan without good reason. He knew that the odds were against him. Perhaps his horse was swifter but he had to do something to even the odds. As he moved towards the starting place he patted the rump of his opponent's horse. At the same time he slid his hand beneath the saddle and placed a sharp piece of flint there. The race began as the crowd yelled their support and encouragement. The younger man shot into the lead showing confidence and skill. Omar's horse which was strong and well bred from a prize Arab stallion, showed the staying power of his breed but Omar's weight had slowed the horse down in comparison. As they drew near the line of flags at the finishing line something happened to the young man's horse. It bucked and threw off his rider. Omar rode past in triumph.

His challenger was shaken but not hurt, accepting that he had been beaten in front of his tribesmen. It would not be acceptable to push his case further. Tinan was unmoved and not really interested that this had been done because of her, but that night when she was helping to pack up, she heard the whispers of the other women in the household.

'We will have to watch that one with the blue eyes. She is still so young but she has a strange power over the men in this tribe.'

'Yes, you are right. I wonder if she has been circumcised yet. She is of the age but our master doesn't hold with that custom so perhaps it is not likely to happen.'

'The master need not have anything to do with it. I was done when I was younger than her by a woman who visited all the caravans in the area to perform this religious practice.'

'Maybe so, but it would only annoy him. If today is any guide, he obviously has a keen interest in her future.'

Tinan discussed this conversation with Takamat, incensed to think that such a barbaric custom existed.

'Don't worry my dear friend you are safe here. Omar obviously likes to have his women intact until the time that he decides to deflower them.'

'Do you think that he has that event in mind for me?' asked Tinan.

'It is quite possible as he often looks at you with undisguised interest, and you are of the age when he would feel entitled to do this.'

'But Takamat, he already has a harem of women to use. I find him quite repulsive.'

'That doesn't mean anything. He is the master and we are the slaves. That is how we must live our lives.'

Tinan's eyes glowed fiercely as she tossed back her long black hair and said.

'No, I will not. I will run away before I submit to his lust.' The next day when the caravan prepared to move out Takamat slowly shuffled past Omar. She noticed that he had removed a small leather purse from around his neck and was holding something in his hand which glistened in the sun. As she was walking on a direct route towards him, she couldn't avoid looking at what he held. It was a small round object with a silver replica of a fish which shimmered and moved towards the sun. When he realized that she had seen it, he hastily closed his fist around it and lowered his hand. Takamat wouldn't have thought much about it until he did that. It seemed as if he was trying to hide something. She told Tinan about the strange moving fish in Omar's purse, and they both agreed to be observant if and when he consulted it again. Omar's journey had taken them away from Egypt into Libya, and he was still moving west. He knew exactly where they were and his compass was the reason.

Many years ago when Omar visited Cairo he met with a Greek in a waterside café where they soon became drinking buddies. Of course both boasted of their many adventures, but nothing which Omar related could match his friend's tale about his guiding star. One night after a heavy bout of imbibing, Omar challenged the Greek to prove his story by showing him this magic guide. After a little fumbling the Greek produced a small leather pouch from around his neck pulling out a round cylinder with a tiny profile of a silver fish. The head of this fish swiveled and always pointed in the same direction. It didn't matter if it was turned to face another direction, it always returned to the same position. Omar was astounded but more importantly he realized that if he had this magic guide, he would never get lost in the desert. It was an object worth having and perhaps even dying for! Still he needed to know more about it.

'It must be some sort of trick. Why does it always move like that?'

'This little sliver of silver has magnetic properties which have been used by sailors for many years. It is made from something called lodestone which always aligns itself to point in the direction of the North Star, no matter how many times you turn it away, it will still swing back to that bearing.'

Omar held his tongue. He now knew enough, so he said goodnight to his drinking partner. They turned in opposite directions but Omar pulled out his dagger, crept up to his companion where he quickly cut his throat before the poor man had realised what had happened. He groped at the Greek's neck for the cord and pouch cutting the leather thong which held it. It was dark and deserted, so nobody saw him roll the dead man into the river. Nobody would question another death from a drunken bout in this area. It was not uncommon for the river to become a graveyard. The crocodiles were excellent scavengers making quick work of such carcasses.

Now Omar moved back and forth at whim. He knew with certain confidence that his journeys were always arranged to his benefit alone. Although not a wealthy man, he had a considerable flock of sheep, goats and camels for sale as his caravan moved across the Trans-Saharan trade route. He was a business man of some repute but he had to pay Berber guides to ensure safe passage from fellow desert nomads. It was on such an occasion after the conclusion of business that Omar felt his attention turn to Tinan. He had given the other women permission to go to the local market place to buy some new rugs and other household necessities.

Knowing that he was alone with the exception of that ugly woman with the shrivelled leg, he called Tinan to come to him. When she entered, he pulled down the tent flap and asked her to sit down on one of the many cushions in the room. She did this with some trepidation because his movements seemed contrived and stealthy. He took her hand roughly, clamping a slave bracelet onto her wrist and attaching it to a tent pole. She knew that the time for losing her virginity was upon her. There was nothing that she could do about it. She hissed at him, tried to move away, but he threw her down again on the nearest cushions. He had already removed just about all of his clothing and was now almost ready to take her.

As he lowered himself on top of her his heavy body almost winded her, but that was nothing compared with his hands which seemed to have a mind of their own. He slapped her twice across her face then pulled on her thick hair, painfully jerking back her neck. Ripping off her robe he rasped her tender breasts with calloused hands. His arms which were encased with bracelets, scratched and drew blood from her belly and her chest as he moved them downwards with such force. Screaming at this vile attack only seemed to make him more excited. She viewed his large extended member with horror as he moved it closer to the private part of her body. He then began to nibble at her breasts, making weird grunting noises. By now she was aware that she couldn't escape from this terrible nightmare. Just before she closed her eyes in futile resistance, she felt a heated and searing pain in her vagina as he rammed himself into her. Neither of them noticed that Takamat had crept under the tent's flap as she suspected that Omar had chosen this day for the rape of Tinan. She picked up Omar's dagger from the cushion where he had flung it and drove it with all her strength into the left side of his back straight into his heart. Omar had not time to ejaculate, but when she saw his dagger imbedded in his back, Tinan managed to bring up her knees and kick him away from her. Then she began to sob and shudder with the aftermath of this outrage. Takamat knew that they had little time before his body would be found. She spoke urgently to her friend.

'I know that you're in an acutely fragile condition, and we can't dispose of his huge body, so there is only one thing that we can do. If you want to stay alive, we have to get away from here as quickly as possible. I can get some of the women's clothes for us to wear. We can cover our faces with the long turban scarves to avoid recognition. There is a little money in his small table for us to purchase food, but I am afraid that our only chance is to ride on the camels to escape. I will attend to your injuries later, but Tinan you have to be brave and accept the pain which you are feeling now. That is nothing in comparison to what would be done to us if we fall into the hands of this household. Believe me. The women would torture us in ways which are indescribable. Even circumcision wouldn't be as bad as what they are capable of doing.'

'Yes,' sobbed Tinan. 'You are right, but before you find those clothes please remove the little leather pouch from around his neck. I shall keep it as a reminder of this terrible day. You will find the key to my bracelet on the cushion with his discarded clothing. Please hurry!' Tinan realised the danger that they both were in as a steely resolve came over her.

Allowing Takamat to dress her, they both left the tent through the back entrance. The camels bent down for this as they had been taught, and there was a small ladder to allow Tinan to mount but as she was bleeding and hurt she struggled to move into a sitting position. When this was done they headed away from the caravan and this town as inconspicuously as possible. The sun was sinking but they had no time to stop for food or shelter. Takamat had managed to pick up some dates and dried fruit which she packed with her salves and herbs into a small woven basket. She included a cup, plate and a knife, but this was for later in their journey. For now they had to put as much distance between dead Omar and themselves. They really had little idea where they were heading, but they knew that the setting sun was the direction of the Great Sahara desert. As they rode on through the night Takamat heard little muffled whimpers coming from her friend, but as long as she hung onto the pommel of the camel's saddle Tinan was safe from falling. By morning, Takamat was weary but happy to see that there was no sign of them being followed. She caught up to Tinan and suggested that perhaps they had been lucky this once. When she raised her head Takamat was stunned. Tinan's face was black and blue and one of her eyes was so swollen that it had closed.

Not being one to dwell on the negative side of their situation, she informed Tinan that they could have a little of the food, and then they must find a settlement where they could rest and revive. After this brief stop they both continued to the next rise in the sand dunes. There was no sign of habitation to be seen but there were some palm trees close by to a rocky outcrop which might offer some shelter. They made it by noon when the sun became their new enemy. Fortunately Takamat managed to find a cave amongst the rocky terrain. She gently helped Tinan to dismount and walk to this cool haven.

She tethered the camels, removed their saddles and saddlecloths which she used to lay on the ground for Tinan to rest upon. Her reward was Tinan's smile as she lowered herself onto the covered ground. Takamat gave her a little of the food, and then went outside to search for water. This took some time, and she would have had trouble finding her way back to the cave except for the camels standing nearby. When she entered the cave Tinan was sleeping so she went out again to explore the area. This was not easy as her withered leg was not made for walking on rough uneven ground. She found herself slipping on the loose stones but that was preferable to what they had just left behind them. Tinan awoke with a start. She realised that she was alone, but the aches and pains came back with a dreadful rush, so she moved her body very gingerly. Takamat returned with her report.

'There seems to be no sign of any human civilization in this area so I feel that we are safe here for some time until you regain your strength. In the meantime I have found a little water for you, and I have brought some oil and salves for your aching body. Please allow me to attend to them for you.'

Tinan lay down whilst Takamat gently lifted the cloth around the parts of her abused body. She recoiled in disbelief as she saw the scratches and abrasions over her chest and belly. In some places the blood had adhered to the cloth so it was going to be painful to remove one from the other.

'My dearest one this is not going to be easy for me to do, but you will have to bear a little discomfort whilst I mix some oil with the salves and gently massage them into your broken skin. Where the cloth has stuck to the wounds, I may have to cut it away.'

Takamat was as gentle as she could be attending to these injuries trying not to show the emotion which she felt about this intimacy between herself and this beautiful young woman who had not deserved this type of violence. She saw the soft swell of Tinan's lovely full breasts and tried not to admit to any arousal, but this was the first time that she had ever felt like this. Men had shunned her and it was not her place to instigate any other type of advances herself. Tinan began to moan softly as she felt Takamat massaging her belly. Takamat immediately pulled back her hand.

'What's the matter? Have I hurt you?'

'No you have not but after you worked the salve around my breasts and then my belly, I felt a strange flutter in the pit of my stomach. Perhaps I have internal bruising where he entered me.' Tinan said.

'No. that is not the case at all! Please forgive me. What I have done with every good intention has stirred some sensation within you. I can't believe that this could happen after what you have been through. I will go no further but when you have the strength to walk outside and urinate I will give you some more water and a cloth to remove the blood which has dried there. You can do this without my help.'

Tinan looked at her friend: the woman who had saved her life was now acting a little strangely. So be it. They still had a long way to go and it was obvious that they needed each other to do this. The rest of the day went quickly. She managed to walk outside without any assistance and attend to the cleansing of the private part of her body. Then she returned to the saddle cloth and lay down to sleep.

Takamat said nothing, as she knew that tomorrow would see them on their way. Tinan's aching body should be rested enough to continue their journey.

As dawn crept through the cave's opening Takamat rose to go outside, but her eyes widened as she realized that three men dressed in flowing robes and turbans stood in her way. Easing herself to where Tinan lay sleeping, she gently shook her. By this time the men had moved forward and had confirmed that the two women were alone. One of the men shook Tinan and lifted her to her feet. This effort was greeted with a few grunts as her arms and body were still a little tender, but she knew that she had to show no fear.

Recognising their language, Takamat knew that these men were Tuareg slave traders, so she said nothing. They indicated to the two females to gather up their saddles and extra goods and they instructed them to mount their camels. She hadn't tried to hide them. The camels had led these men to the cave but it was too late now. Glancing at Tinan she knew that she was not too comfortable but she was managing to hide it well. Their camels were roped to the other three and they were led to the men's destination in a caravan procession. They were given water and some food as they travelled on a journey which took nearly all day.

On arrival at the camp the two women were separated. Because she was small and slim they must have been assumed that she was younger than she looked, so Takamat was put in a tent with younger girls. Tinan was taken to the women's tent but this all seemed so different to her experience with Omar's family. These women who were unveiled were more respected. They did not cower or carry themselves like slaves which suited Tinan very well. At heart she was proud and arrogant so she knew that she would fit in perfectly with this domestic arrangement. Right from the start, she was disdainful and superior, an attitude which seemed to be acceptable by the females of this clan.

Her first request was to have a bath, and although her language was not perfect, she made herself understood. A rather small metal tub was produced, filled with warm water, and she was given some kind of soap and a cloth towel. As she shed her clothes before the other women, a few gasped at the still obvious signs of bruises and lacerations covering her upper torso, but they respected the silence and lack of concern shown by Tinan. After this was completed, Tinan felt wonderful. She had been rescued from an uncertain fate by these Tuaregs, but she was still mindful that they made their living from selling human slaves. She knew that her resolve was strong enough to face most things now.

The clan gathered for dining and socializing, where Tinan was made welcome, and she relished this role as if she had been born into it. Their leader was a handsome man called Salaman, who was eager to hear all about Tinan and why she had become lost in the desert. She skillfully spoke about having been kidnapped from Pharaoh's Palace in Egypt where she was sold to slavers. She did not elaborate as to where they had lived and for how long, only that they had managed to escape.

When this meeting was over, she insisted that her maid Takamat be released into her company to attend her. This was also acceptable as being a natural request from a high born lady. The lady named Mushtari, was the undisputed head of this company. She had noted the marks over Tinan's body, but decided to bide her time before she questioned her about them. Apart from her carriage and forthright manner, Mushtari dressed in the finest of clothes and wore beautiful silver jewelry. Her word was law, and even some of the men were subservient to her, which surprised Tinan.

TINAN HINAN

She favoured Tinan's company and showed no jealousy when her husband and some of the other males would seek Tinan's comments on various matters. The new addition to this household had many talents. Not only did she speak with some intelligence but she had little inhibitions, offering to sing and entertain at the various celebrations.

Although the songs were Egyptian, Tinan had worked out a rough translation so that they were understood by all present. Pipes and drums were added to this performance as well as the participation of the women's rhythmic clapping. This became a regular activity as Tinan encouraged the younger women to use bells and flutes. Her achievements did not go un-noticed by Salaman, who considered the possibility of marriage for Tinan. He discussed this with his wife who accepted her husband's opinion in the matter, but she didn't mention this to Tinan as she knew that this had to be handled with delicate diplomacy.

A wedding was to take place in a nearby town, to which Salaman and his family were invited. This included everyone, as all hands were needed to help with dressing, cleansing, hair styling and many other necessities before appearing at the family's tent for the nuptials. Tinan was allowed to borrow a beautiful blue dress from Mushtari, which complimented her stunning blue eyes. Her hair was braided and adorned with borrowed silver jewelry which was neatly woven through her black hair. She could have outshone the bride, but she waited in the background until after the ceremony, when she was asked to sing for the wedding party.

She chose a slow love song, swaying with the rhythm as her nimble fingers plucked at a harp. The words resonated with all present as she sang.

'Come my beloved help me clear today of past regret and future fear. Slave or sultan we can find the key which helps us join the Thee and Me.'

Takamat handled the castanets with great ability and the audience was most enthusiastic when the song ended. Salaman and Mushtari nodded their approval with a new layer of respect for Tinan.

The married couple's tent was festooned with flags waving outside in the breeze, and with richly embroidered cushions and draped curtains inside. All were made welcome for the feast which was to last for days. Salaman had arranged for his cousin Nizam to meet Tinan. This proved to be a meeting of mutual dislike. Nizam was proud, dull and overbearing, all traits which did not impress Tinan. She was haughty, self opinionated and had a wicked sense of humour. She had guessed what might be at the bottom of the attention which was being shown by Nizam, so she waited until they had returned to her own tent before she discussed this with Mushtari.

'I know that you expect me to be married as I am of an age where this is normal, but if you recall how I came to you two years ago, I was covered with the scars of a brutal rape. I have forgotten this awful abusive treatment of my body, but my heart has not.'

'We love you like a daughter and we know that you carry a unique intelligence in those lovely blue eyes, but you will need the protection of a man with strong tribal connections to provide for you and take care of you in the future years. Nizam could be that man.'

'Your words are meant with my best interests but please give me some time to adjust to this idea. I have always carried the hope that perhaps I will meet a man and love him as he loves me, and I don't feel that with Nizam.'

Mushtari smiled at this idealistic approach confessing to Tinan.

'How do you think that I met my husband? My parents had made arrangements for my betrothal long before I met Salaman.

They wisely believed that we would be suitable for each other, and before we wed we did find love in each other's eyes.'

'I am pleased for you. Anyone can see that you are perfectly matched, but I cannot see or feel that this will happen in my case.'

Mushtari discussed this reluctance on the part of Tinan with her husband, but he scoffed at her feelings. It was time for him to have a talk with Tinan.

'You have been part of our family for some time now and you've grown to know the ways of the Tuareg people. Unlike some other tribes, we welcome and allow the strength of our women. It is rare to find any marital problems. As you would have noticed, Mushtari makes most of the decisions pertaining to our household. It is because of this situation, I feel that you could handle your own household happiness with my cousin Nizam.'

'But Salaman he doesn't even like me. His conversation is boring, he doesn't seem to know how to smile, and I felt totally intimidated by his presence.'

'Not so, my little one. As a man of our tribe he has a certain position which would never allow any show of public affection or great interest in a woman, even one as lovely as you are. He has spoken privately of his opinion of you, holding you in great esteem. His hesitation to show this is because you were both at a celebration, where it would not be seemly for him to make advances which you possibly would have liked. I can assure you that with a chaperone for both of you, in another setting you would see a totally different man.'

'Thank you for your advice, I shall take some time to consider this, and we will talk again.' said Tinan as she withdrew.

She walked outside where she found Takamat tending the camels. Salaman's proposition had left her with the need for an unbiased opinion.

'I feel terribly alone and confused. Both Salaman and Mushtari have suggested that I am of marriageable age. They think that their cousin is a suitable husband for me. I have no feelings for this man, yet he seems to want to take me for his wife.'

Takamat was a little flustered as this confession, but she knew what was best for Tinan.

'Why do you hesitate? Love is only something which we sing about. That isn't a lasting passion or real life. As you were perhaps the daughter of a slave, you could rise to a wonderful position as the wife of this man. You deserve security and I notice that the Tuaregs are not cruel or dominating with their female counterparts. Your life could be exactly as you wish it to be.'

'Thank you my dear friend. Perhaps it would be suitable for me to get to know him better just to see how I feel about him.'

After this conversation, Tinan went to Mushtari, confirmed that she would like to meet Nizam with the intention of getting to know him a little better. Mushtari was pleased, and arranged a chaperone to sit in the same tent when Nizam came to call. He mostly spoke about himself, sending her shy glances as he searched for some spark of interest in her eyes. This was not there until he told her about his beautiful Arab horses. When she heard this Tinan changed her facial expression and asked him.

'Do you have any horses which would be suitable for me to ride?'

He was not expecting to hear this from a woman, as this was highly unusual. Horses were kept in readiness for defence during the frequent inter-tribal fights. They were considered a man's symbol of success and pride.

'But women don't ride horses. It would be difficult for you to learn,' he said. Tinan gave him a defiant stare and said.

'If I can ride a camel, I can learn to ride a horse.' The chaperone in the background let out a guffaw which quickly changed into a coughing fit. Nizam was nonplussed as he recognised that this woman was feisty and brave. She would give him fine sons after they were married so he agreed.

'I do have a gentle mare which would be ideal. I shall lead her here with my own stallion and we can ride together if Salaman approves.'

Tinan smiled as she looked carefully at this young man. He seemed very young perhaps only in his early twenties. His unlined face showed no signs of hardship, his shoulders were broad and his waist was slim but her intuition told her that he was a little in awe of her. It was important for her to learn to ride a horse as they were speedy and intelligent creatures. This would give her time to make up her mind about her future with Nizam. Salaman had no objections as long as another male rider was with them. After all he had to follow the protocol of their culture. His cousin certainly had riding skills which even Tinan would recognise. The first day Nizam introduced her to horse riding, he could see that she had a natural seat and an enthusiasm which matched his own love of horses.

This became a regular occurrence as Tinan found herself actually looking forward to her lessons with Nizam. Unfortunately her sense of her own importance nearly had serious consequences.

One day when he arrived with both horses, Tinan insisted that she was ready to mount the black stallion. Nothing which Nizam said made any difference, so she was hoisted onto his back. The horse recognized a different rider and one with little or no experience, so it took off at a gallop. The chaperone who was Salaman's eldest son took off immediately after her, so Nizam had no recourse but to ride the small grey mare after them both.

The result was inevitable as Tinan was thrown, just missing a pile of rocks. Salaman's son Habib, was there to lift her body away from the prancing stallion. At that precise moment when he looked into her eyes they both fell instantly in love. By the time Nizam had reached them Tinan could not contain her laughter to see this tall man astride a little stocky mare.

Nizam was not amused, showing obvious concern for her. She felt a little ashamed for making such a request when it could have had a much worse outcome. That night after she was pronounced fit and well, Tinan took aside her friend to reveal the happenings of the day. She told her that when she was in the arms of Salaman's eldest son Habib she felt an instant charge of something inexplicable happening to her.

'Well now, how does that compare with your feelings about Nizam?'

'They are non-existent, except to say that I am sorry for being so impetuous and putting his precious stallion in danger. He seems so devoid of any romantic expression that I feel my life would be boring and worthless if I married him.'

'Perhaps you had better have a chat with Mushtari. Habib is her son and she knows him better than anyone.'

'Yes Takamat, as usual you always have the right answers.'

Tinan didn't have to bring up the subject as Habib had already spoken to his parents about his feelings for her. When she approached them they were already well informed about what had happened.

'This makes things a little difficult for us to comment, because as much as we love our eldest son, and would rejoice in his happiness, he hardly knows you at all. The same goes for you. Although Nizam has not formally become betrothed to you, we feel that our words have given him an understanding and the right of expectation concerning his future with you.'

'But Nizam has not asked me to marry him yet. I know that you wouldn't force me to wed him against my will.'

'No, but our son hasn't asked you either. Even if he feels smitten with you, it would be against the family's honour if we simple ignored Nizam's request for your hand.'

'But can't you see, I feel the same way about Habib, in a way that I have never felt about any man. Please justify our feelings with your understanding.'

That night Tinan heard loud and angry words coming from Salaman's section of the tent. She became afraid for Habib.

'How can you feel that a passing moment which you shared physically holding her in your arms can be called anything more than a human connection? That is not love and you are foolish to convert a simple situation into anything like that,' roared Salaman.

'I fell in love with her the very first day that we found her in that cave. She was afraid, distressed and still beautiful. I have watched and listened to her as she has moved amongst our people with her kindness, wisdom and humour. She carries herself like a princess, and I would die for her.'

'You may have to do just that my son. If we agree to your request to marry her we will be inviting all sorts of trouble from Nizam as well as his side of the family. He will feel shamed and insulted by our change of attitude and perhaps with good reason. I will have to give this much thought.'

When Tinan heard this passionate avowal from Habib's lips, her heart soared. Nizam had never showed such emotion whereas Habib had indicated his true and deepest feelings which strongly resonated with her own.

Mushtari was just as concerned. Her eldest son was well loved by her, but the family's honour was at stake and she couldn't help but worry. Habib was love sick, of that there was no doubt, but was it something which he could put behind him if Tinan wed Nizam. Both of Nizam's parents had passed away, so there was no appeal or discussion with any senior members of that household. Salaman and Mushtari had to face him and try to use some skill to appease him.

At first Nizam was understanding when Salaman indicated that Tinan was not interested in marrying him. Despite their mutual love of horses they were not ideally suited. Nizam was still young and healthy. In time he would certainly find a more suitable bride. He went along with this line of thinking, but when Salaman told him that Tinan had fallen in love with their son, this completely changed his attitude. Now his pride was severely wounded, and he had to take steps to remedy this.

'If she doesn't love me that makes no difference as I would still marry her anyway, but if she has chosen another over me, I have to retain my respect and honour. Even though he is your son and a member of my clan, I cannot let this insult go unpunished. I will have to resort to fighting him to the death.'

Mushtari took a deep intake of breath as the tears filled her eyes. She couldn't see that any love was worth the upheaval and possible loss of life that might ensue, but this was not her decision so she said nothing. When his parents called Habib into their presence and told him about their meeting with Nizam, he was not unduly worried. He expected that something like this would happen. The fire in his heart for Tinan burned too brightly to consider any other action. If there had to be a fight for her, he was willing. Although Habib was a few years older than Nizam, he knew his Father's younger cousin very well. He hoped that something might happen to alter the attitude which Nizam had adopted. The other consideration was that a question of honour was usually settled with swords. Nizam was the senior male in his household, but he hadn't had much experience with swords, whereas Habib had. Salaman had encouraged his three sons to safely use them, honing their skills as they matured. Even today Salaman's business interests concerned the sale and transport of camels. If there were skirmishes between the tribes, his sons had to be able to defend their livelihood. This was not the case with Nizam and he was painfully aware of his shortcoming in this field.

Salaman spoke to his other sons as he tried to explain that this would not be a fair fight because Nizam would be totally out of his league, in pitting his sword against Habib. He also went to visit Nizam and suggested that perhaps there could be some other way to resolve this confrontation. His young cousin was well aware that he would be the underdog in this fight, but apart from his magnificent stable of horses, he had little else in his life.

'Perhaps you could feign an injury and retire before you are badly hurt.' Salaman suggested.

'No my dear cousin, I will not do that. I shall be brave and if I die, my family will not suffer the shame which Tinan has brought upon me.'

A time and a place were prepared for this event, but very few attended. Habib took a long glance at Tinan as she waved goodbye from the tent, and he was ready. His brothers accompanied him to an oasis on the outskirts of a town, where a tent was erected for this contest. When Nizam arrived with some other male friends, he almost looked disinterested, but that all changed when they removed their turbans and outer robes. He took an instant slash before

Habib had finished taking off his outer clothes, which was probably just as well.

This only served to annoy Habib as he knew that there were rules to fighting a duel of honour that his cousin was ignoring. He was angry, but still in control, so he played around a little, getting to know just how good Nizam's sword skills were. When he had enough of this ducking from Nizam's moves, he decided to end it quickly. He had no intention of killing his adversary, although he knew that he could, so he wounded him by using a wide sweeping stroke aimed at his right arm which held Nizam's sword. A red patch of blood erupted from the cut through his shirt, but it was only a surface wound. When the sword clattered to the floor, Habid held his own at Nizam's throat, but he smiled as he shook his head and lowered his weapon. But Nizam was not finished. He went to pick up his own discarded sword with his left hand, but Habib's two brothers pinned his arms. Habib spoke.

'Your honour has been met with the debt to your family now paid. Let that be the end of this, as you are my kinsman and I have no desire to abuse that connection.'

Nizam's passion was aroused for possibly the first time in his life, because he knew that he was outclassed by this man. He spat out the words.

'There will never be any friendly connection between my family and yours. You have beaten me today. Even if you become the bridegroom of that devil with the blue eyes, I and my family will never forget what has happened.'

When the three brothers returned home to everyone's relief, Habib informed his father of what had transpired and what Nizam had said.

'That is a great shame, because that should have been the end of it. It sounds as if Nizam will not forgive and forget, but far worse, he may instill the same hatred into his own clan, which could produce a vendetta against us. This would become an ongoing war with more blood letting and murder'.

When Tinan heard that Habib was back, unhurt, she wanted to see him. Once again she was warned against showing any kind of public affection, but this was too much for her. She ran to his tent bursting in without an invitation. Habib was deep in conversation with his brothers but although he was happy to see her reaction, he had to obey the rules. She was gently but firmly removed from the tent with Habib's disappointment showing in his face. It won't be too long before I can take her in my arms, he thought.

Mushtari was overjoyed to see that her son was unhurt, but she also took counsel from her husband and knew that this day's work could have serious consequences. After discussing it they decided that it would be wise to dismantle their tents and move away before any more trouble came to pass. Habib was irate.

'How can you run away from him? He means nothing to us and even though he made veiled threats against our family, this would never happen. I can't believe that you would consider behaving in a cowardly fashion after I beat him in a sword fight.'

Mushtari could see that her son was annoyed with the news, but she had to think about all of her family which included her husband, three sons, two daughters and five servants as well as two male slaves. The risk was too great. Anyway Tuaregs roamed across the desert at their whim so now would be a good time to celebrate Habib's marriage in another part of the country. They had distant relatives near the border of Algeria, where her husband had agreed to transport a large shipment of camels. It was settled. Tinan was informed that her marriage would take place in a few weeks after they had left this camp site. They knew of her genuine concern for Habib, so they allowed her to spend time in his tent with another female chaperone.

Tinan did not want to discuss the past, but she was very interested in their future. He softened in her presence and although he had to be discreet with his obvious desire for her, took her hand and kissed it lovingly.

'My dearest one, my lips are locked together upon your hand which seals my fate. Within your heavenly eyes I can see reflected the blooming flower of our love. It will live and blossom. Neither desert wind nor sun will wither it. You are my love for all eternity.'

Tinan's breathing grew rapidly. It took all her will power to stop from throwing herself into his arms. She lifted her head, but half lowered her lashes over her tear filled eyes as she controlled her passion.

'Habib, you are my strength and my weakness. I will journey with you to taste from the Well of Life. A flower only has a certain life, the same can be said of fruit of the vine, but we will taste the joys and pleasures of our union and drink from it deeply.'

Although their love was confessed within earshot of a chaperone, her silent tears attested that this was truly a love match. She gently coughed to remind them that it was time to part. Within a few days when all the camels for sale were delivered to Salaman, the time had come to dismantle the tents and move on.

Tinan had confessed her love for Habib to Takamat. Now her excitement about the coming marriage was evident in her every word and movement. The move to another place to begin their life which included Takamat in their household, was about to start.

'I am happy for you. I appreciate that you would want me to still be involved in your life. You are my mistress as well as my friend, and I wouldn't want to be anywhere else where you are not.'

'Thank you Takamat. I would like you to have this old leather purse and its contents, which I have worn on my belt for years. We both went through this ordeal together, but now that I am to be married, I want to bring nothing of the past to our new life.'

She took the small purse from Tinan, opened it and removed the little circular object. She watched in amazement as the head of the silver fish moved towards one direction, no matter where she turned it or where she stood with it.

'Tinan this is truly a wondrous object. We could have done with its help when we fled from Omar's tent into the desert. I believe that it will point the way to a particular part of this country and will never waver. Its benefit could be enormous to someone who becomes lost in the desert. Now that I think about it, Omar must have consulted it regularly when he was on the move. It would have kept him going in the right direction, no matter what the visibility was around him.'

'You have discovered the secret of this little fish, so please guard it carefully and wear it at all times. I believe that it is amazing and valuable, but I don't want it to fall into any other hands.'

'It is safe with me, my lady,' replied Takamat.

It was time to have a talk with Mushtari, as Tinan thought it prudent to do this before the caravan's departure and her upcoming marriage. She had confided in her regarding the terrible events which led to her rape and physical abuse, but this was not ever discussed with Habib. Tinan was concerned that he would be expecting his wife to be a virgin, and might be very disappointed. Mushtari put those fears to rest. She took Tinan's hands in her own and spoke gently to her.

'You have nothing to fear my daughter, because after Habib found you in that cave so obviously in distress and pain, he knew that you both were running away from some disturbing event. He told us that he felt you had been violated. You must remember that your face was cut and swollen. Your movements on that day would have indicated further damage to your body. It wasn't until later when you confirmed what had happened that I took him aside and explained that his fears were correct. Habib loves you as you were the day that you came into his life, so have no concern on that account.'

Tinan felt her emotions run high. She could no nothing to stay the tears which fell, but this conversation was enough to give her confidence to face the man who would be her husband very soon.

The next day the camp was struck, the tents rolled and folded and placed onto the camels' backs. All the household items were treated in a similar fashion. Salaman ordered all the camels to be connected to each other so that they moved out in one long procession.

When they neared the area known as the Ahaggar Mountains, Mushtari chose a place which was situated in a desert wadi. It was once used as a settlement by Roman legions which had used the various forts and outposts to facilitate the trade of gold, ivory, spices and wheat. There had been cultivation and signs of suitable land for growing crops. This would be the place where Habib and Tinan would celebrate their marriage, so the preparations began almost immediately.

There was a small population of Tuaregs living around these mountains. When the news had spread about the forthcoming wedding celebrations, messengers were sent to invite them. Salaman believed that his house was a poor home without guests, and he encouraged as many as he could to share the happy festivities for his eldest son's marriage.

Tinan and Habib were wed in accordance to their custom. She wore a loose unencumbered dark blue dress which was embellished with hand embroidery in black and red. Although Tinan had no dowry to display, Mushtari gave her a headdress which was specially padded with many coins sewn on it. She wanted Tinan to have some wealth of her own, so she gave her new daughter some beautiful silver bangles and a very unusual silver necklace with pearls. When the feasting, singing and dancing had ended the guests departed. The time had come for

Tinan and Habib to make their way to the bridal chamber. Mushtari had fitted it out with silk cushions, curtains and lovely braziers from which coloured and perfumed candles glowed. These were things which she had gathered from her travels as well as the markets she visited, in the hope that she could present to her son something really special on his wedding night. There were bowls of apricots, dates, nuts and other fruit, which were discreetly placed for their enjoyment.

They were not disturbed for two days. This time was so incredible for Tinan in a way which she never could have imagined. Habib had undressed her slowly never taking his eyes from hers enjoying her every expression as she thrilled to his gentle touch. She lay down on the couch and closed her eyes. He knew that she had been violently used, but today he wanted her to be the one to instigate this introduction to sexual pleasure. When he had undressed himself, he knelt on the floor beside her bed and began to kiss her softly. This aroused her immediately and she opened her eyes, wondering why he had not come to lay down beside her. He said.

'You are the moon and the stars. I am only your husband who worships you completely, so I am going to kiss every part of your body before we consummate our union. I will bring you to such a point of ecstasy that you will be begging me to join you.'

She knew that it must have taken tremendous control on his part, but he had inflamed her completely with his amorous technique that her body was trembling with longing and a compelling craving for him. When he knew that he had aroused her to that point he lay down beside her began to kiss her passionately. She was drifting into a world that had no night or day. All she knew was that her body was screaming for his. She began moving against him with her legs apart waiting for him, longing to be his completely. Habib knew that the time was right and he didn't disappoint her. They moved together in a rhythmic display of human sexual performance, and on reaching that perfect pinnacle, were both filled with rapture and delight. He was a considerate lover, but also a very good one. He brought her to climax many times over those days and their intimacy was cemented with physical intercourse and mental stimulation.

Tinan knew why she loved this man, and also how she would cherish their future together. After they emerged from their marriage bed, Salaman told Tinan that both she and Habib would be given a tent with all the items to set up their household.

'It is the custom that a man and wife should begin married life together on their own. We will stay in this area, but unless you need to see us, I don't expect that it will happen for a while. You need this time to get to know each other and to enjoy the bliss that all newlyweds deserve.'

So Tinan and Habib left the company of Salaman and Mushtari. Habib still worked with his brothers in tending to the sheep and goats, but he wasn't asked to take any long treks with the camels for a while.

Takamat stayed with Salaman's household, which she understood was for the best, but she missed her mistress very much and would often find ways to meet Tinan at the market-place.

After a few months, Tinan was overjoyed to find that she was pregnant. This was one of those times when they visited his parents to make the announcement. Salaman couldn't have been happier. Mushtari knew that childbirth wasn't always easy the first time, but she was positive and happy for them both. As Tinan's body began to swell, she asked Habib if she could have her maid Takamat to come and live with them. He agreed to this, knowing that it would make both women very happy.

Habib had organised a camel's side saddle to be made for Tinan when the walk to the market became too much. She enjoyed the gentle swaying motion which calmed her, as well as the invigorating fresh air. It was a weekly outing which she looked forward to with Takamat as her companion.

One afternoon when the two women had gone to the market, the tent of Salaman and Mushtari was invaded and ransacked by some hostile nomads.

Many of the household items were broken and smashed. The tent was cut with swords, the sheep and goats were driven away by men who had their faces hidden in dark turbans. Unfortunately Habib and his brothers were away attending to business, so they arrived back when it was all over. There didn't seem to be any reason for this attack as Salaman and his family were law abiding citizens and hadn't been guilty of bad business dealings. Habib invited his parents and their household to join him and Tinan in their tent until a new one could be found. This was a happy domestic arrangement for all, as the men with the exception of Salaman were usually gone most of the day anyway, so Mushtari spent time with her new daughter and awaited the arrival of their first grandchild.

It came to Habib's attention that the raid carried out on his parent's tent was the work of a kinsman. Nizam and two of his male relatives decided to take their revenge out on Habib, but when they couldn't find him, they destroyed his parent's tent instead together with all their belongings. When his brothers heard this they decided to follow Nizam into the desert, but this action was seen as foolhardy by Salaman. He counselled patience.

'We need to think this through, as rushing headlong after these men could turn out to be a disaster. They could be expecting you to follow them and set up an ambush. There is no way that we even know which direction they took so we need to make some enquiries before we take action.'

Salaman was not opposed to handing out some coins for information. He was told that three men who had been seen leaving town on that day were led by a tall man riding a magnificent black stallion. They were heading for the surrounding mountains where there were large caves big enough to hide men and their horses. This made sense to Salaman because he suspected that Nizam would come back to finish what he had started. The mountains would put him within a handy distance to do that. Habib did a lot of thinking about this problem, because he knew that somehow it was his to solve. He didn't want to involve his brothers, because then it would become an endless vendetta: family against family. He told Tinan that he had worked out a plan to rid them of this evil menace. Of course she was not satisfied with this, begging him for more details. He did not elaborate, except to say that 'I will arrange it.' She found Takamat and told her about this conversation.

'I fear for Habib's life. He has told me that he is going to do something to rid us all of this overhanging threat from Nizam. He possibly will not take his brothers with him, so the odds against him succeeding are becoming less. I am guessing that this will happen soon, but I am asking you to inform the two male slaves to watch our tent day and night. If Habib leaves alone they must follow him and possibly help if it becomes necessary. I cannot interfere myself as this would be wrong, but he will be up against an evil group this time, and I dont trust Nizam at all. I will beg my husband to reconsider this foolishness, but I know that it would be useless as his pride would not allow him to see reason.'

Takamat nodded her agreement, and went to find the two male slaves. They were both natives who were strong and fit, but probably not well versed in the art of sword play. She gave them the coins from Tinan's wedding head dress in appreciation as well as a dagger each from Habib's weapon drawer with strict instructions for secrecy.

'The mistress doesn't want to involve the whole family, as this could lead to a bloodbath of the entire household, including both of you. Her husband wants to settle this matter alone without his brothers, but this would put him at a disadvantage, so you must help him if he needs it. If it should be a challenge between two men, your master will be victorious, but if he is attacked by the others, your assistance would make all the difference.

I suggest that you keep two camels ready as soon as the sun goes down. He will be riding a horse, so you both will have to follow at a cautious distance.'

Two nights later Habib waited until Tinan was asleep. He gently kissed her cheek, and crept out of the tent to where he had saddled his horse. Although he only walked the horse quietly the two slaves were alert and waiting and after a few minutes they mounted the camels and followed him. As soon as he neared the mountain range Habib tethered his horse to a tree and began to scout the area.

Although he had no idea where Nizam might be, he possessed good tracking and hunting skills. He waited until the moon rose to illuminate the mountain tracks and any large opening where horses could be hidden. His eyes gradually became accustomed to the darkness. After about an hour his ears picked up a slight whinny coming from a large opening in the distant rock-face. Habib had every intention to challenge Nizam once again, but he was also hoping to reason with him.

By this time the two slaves had arrived, tethered their camels and slowly crept forward to where they could see Habib and his dagger glinting in the moonlight. Both were silent, as they had no reason to announce their presence at this stage.

When Habib neared the cave, the sound of horses snorting came from the opening. He knew that there would be a guard, so once again he waited until the moon would help him identify the man. Then he dropped to the ground, crawling on his belly until he was behind him. This took more time. Drawing his dagger from its sheath, he put it between his teeth, as he prayed for a quick and silent kill. With one hand over the mouth of the guard, he slashed his throat until the man dropped noiselessly to the ground.

Then Habib removed the blue turban from him and wound it over his own head and face. Before he entered the inner cave, Habib quietly slipped the rope which tethered Nizam's horses, receiving a soft whicker in appreciation. He entered boldly, as any other movement would alert the remaining two men. One was asleep in a corner, whilst Nizam was squatting around a fire drinking tea. His face registered surprise, but he didn't show any fear. He wondered what had happened to the lookout, but didn't waste time dwelling on it.

'I see that you have found us. I was going to pay you a visit at dawn anyway. You've saved me the trouble.'

'This should never have gone this far. Tinan and I are now married. Why do you want to bring more trouble and unhappiness to our family? My parents who have always made you welcome, were undeserving of the damage done to their home. You could leave here tonight and that would be the end of it. If not I will kill you.' When Nizam laughed loudly at this, he awoke the sleeping man who unsheathed his knife. Habib kept an eye on this man who was slowly moving towards him, but he was more interested in Nizam's reply.

'You are so stupid if you think that I care anything about your woman. She means nothing to me. I have come for revenge because you and your family were responsible for shaming me. Now I will close the chapter on this by getting rid of the reason.'

Neither of the men noticed that the three horses had quietly slipped out of the cave's entrance. This was a boon to the two slaves chosen by Tinan who had been given the job of protecting Habib. They knew exactly where he was. Habib realized that there was no point in any further argument, so he withdrew his dagger and walked with intent towards Nizam. Because he was slightly outnumbered Habib kicked the sand and hot coals in front of the fire into Nizam's eyes. This had the desired effect as his opponent went staggering backward, clutching at his face. Unfortunately for Habib, the other man used stealth and cunning. He held a rock in his hand behind his back as he came towards Habib. Although his dagger was raised as Habib ran forward towards Nizam, the other man stood his ground and hurled the rock at Habib's forehead.

This was not enough to seriously wound him, but the blood began to ooze down into his eyes, leaving him with blurred sight. This was the opportunity his attacker was waiting for. He moved quickly, raising his knife and brought it down into Habib's chest.

The two slaves who had crept up to the cave, now rushed in with their blood on fire. Nizam was bending over Habib and whispering something evil, so he was the first one to feel the dagger and its kiss of death. Then both men turned on the killer who having witnessed the size and murderous intent of these two giants, turned and fled. He stumbled in his haste to escape, but it was futile.

His death was the scene of a ghastly massacre, because Habib's slave picked up Nizam's sword and began hacking the man to pieces. A slight cough from the back of the cave alerted the men that Habib must still be alive, so they raced over to him. Taking the turban from Nizam they tried to stem the flow of blood, but it looked to be hopeless. The older of the two said.

'Take the master's horse and ride back. Tell them what has happened here this night, and bring someone who can help him. I will stay here to try to keep him comfortable, but you must hurry.'

Tinan felt her shoulder being shaken, but as she opened her eyes to Takamat she knew that some catastrophe had occurred. She sat upright and knew that because Habib wasn't beside her that he had left to face his fate. Just as she was about to ask Takamat for details, she heard the wailing voice of Mushtari coming from a nearby section of their tent.

'Takamat help me up to dress. I must see Mushtari and I must find my husband.'

Mushtari came in to see her. Her face told it all. She fell to her knees beside Tinan and tried to speak coherently, but it was almost impossible.

'Habib has been fatally wounded. He went alone to face Nizam and although he fought bravely, one of Hizam's men managed to attack your husband with a fatal result.'

'But I don't understand. Was Habib alone? Didn't he have some help?'

Takamat was appalled at this news.

'He went alone without his brothers, but he did have some help from two slaves who were there when it happened. Fortunately they managed to kill Nizam and his kinsman, but the damage had already been done to Habib.'

Mushtari was by now sobbing and tearing at her clothing, but Tinan was calm.

'Is my husband still alive?' she asked.

'Yes I believe so,' said Takamat. 'But that was the case before the slave returned with the terrible news.'

'Takamat, get my camel ready. Make sure that my side saddle is strongly made fast, and then come back and dress me. We will go together. Bring any thing which you think might help him. I must go to him now!'

When she heard this, Mushtari began to wail.

'You cannot go my daughter. You are nearly ready to give birth. The ride wouldn't be easy for you and the shock might affect the baby.'

'Tinan's eyes glowed with determination, but she spoke softly.

'The baby will have to wait. Nothing is going to prevent me from going to see my beloved, and if he is dead or dying, I will not be persuaded to stay here under any circumstances.'

When the camel knelt for Tinan to mount her side saddle, she managed without any trouble. There was a beautiful full moon as Takamat attached a lead to Tinan's camel and then to her own. It was wasted on the two women as they moved slowly towards the terrible scene which awaited them. By this time Salaman and his two sons had arrived by horse. They were not expecting to see two women on camels approaching them.

'Quick, remove that hacked body outside where it can't be seen. This will be hard enough for women to face as it is.' Salaman said.

Both women walked to the cave which by now had been lit with torches.

The scene was like a battlefield with the bloodied body of Nizam and the signs of a fierce struggle where the other man's blood had been shed. Although the knife was still embedded in Habib's chest, the blue turban had been placed over it in the vain hope to stem the bleeding.

Tinan walked in like a Queen, with her head held high and her footsteps firmly controlled. She was helped to sit, by placing a horse rug over a large flat stone which was where she stayed for hours. Takamat wanted to administer some sleeping draught with medicinal properties, but Tinan waved her away. She knew that nothing could help him now. The great loss of blood had drained the colour from his handsome face. She knew that his life was slowly slipping away, and that it couldn't be restored.

'Leave me, all of you,' she said. He is mine in life and in death. I and I alone will make this journey with him to the end.' Takamat's eyes filled with emotion for this brave woman who wanted to experience every moment with the love of her life who was dying. She moved to the back of the cave and found a place to sit. The others slowly filed outside giving Tinan the space that she requested. Then they heard her voice soaring so sweetly and clearly in the night air. It carried over the stones, the sand, the palm trees and the hills. Takamat shivered with fear as she heard the aching intensity of Tinan's loss in her song. She also heard unexpected defiance.

'Heaven filled our lives with desire. Nothing can mar a soul on fire.

A moment's halt to reach the sky, but love for us will never die.'

She sang the rest of the words, holding Habib's hand to her heart. Although his breathing was shallow and his eyes had closed, he managed to squeeze her hand. He heard her as she sang him to his final resting place. When the last breath had left his body, Salaman approached Tinan and tried to prise her hand from Habib's, but she ignored him.

Once again, she turned to the waiting group and told them to leave her alone.

'I have Takamat here with me so leave me until tomorrow. I will wait here with him tonight.'

This seemed like a sensible idea as the early hours of the new day were already dawning. Tinan had made her mind up with a firmness of purpose which would brook no argument. In the flickering torchlight Takamat watched her mistress and her friend become a woman of great strength and resolve. Tinan did not cry then or ever again. It was as if her life-spirit had left her. Something else had taken its place inside her body. She heard Tinan softly singing during what was left of the night, but she didn't disturb her. She had insisted that his life was hers and his death was hers too.

Just before dawn, Takamat went outside to check the camels when she felt something strange in the air. The sand particles outside the cave seemed to be vibrating. Takamat had heard stories about sandstorms which caused this phenomenon: this occurrence was to be greatly feared. Gathering the camels as quickly as she could, she approached Tinan who seemed to be in a trance.

'My lady, please wake up and listen to me. I feel that we are in grave danger, but because of your condition it would be foolish to try to leave and outrun it.'

'What are you talking about? Outrun what?' Tinan snapped.

'A sand storm! The signs are unmistakable. I have brought the camels inside and we will be lucky if we can save them, let alone ourselves. If the storm picks up the surrounding sand dunes, we could be buried alive beneath it. Even if it is not a bad one, it can cause our deaths just by breathing in the dust particles. Our only hope is to get to the back of this cave and cover our bodies and especially our faces with any cloth which we can get hold of. I will tether the camels at the entrance but it will be to sacrifice them to the encroaching sand which will blow and creep inside. Hopefully their bodies will make some sort of a barrier between us and the full force of the storm. No sooner had Takamat uttered the words when a terrible sound shook the ground and the walls of the cave. Then something sounding like an evil apparition came to the entrance wailing like the banshees of hell.

Takamat gathered up the saddlecloth from one of the camels. She helped to move Tinan by placing the saddlecloth beneath her so that she could drag her mistress away from Habib's body to the back of the cave. By this time the camels were loudly protesting, trying to release themselves from their ties, but the full force of the sand and wind began to take its toll. Soon their struggles ceased as they died from asphyxiation.

Tinan had to lie on the hard sandy floor. Takamat covered Tinan's face with the blue turban which had been used to try and stem the flow of Habib's blood. She wound it a few times around the head of her mistress, covering her eyes to prevent her from seeing, before she removed the knife from Habib's chest. She used this to frantically dig a large hole in the firm sandy soil. Then she told Tinan to lie with her face down in this hole, where she would be able to breathe. She wrapped the other saddle blanket around her own face, and dropped down between two large rocks which gave her some protection from the cyclonic sound and the invasive dust. She had no idea how many hours they stayed like this but after a while when the sound subsided a little Takamat heard Tinan grunting. She frowned and prayed that this wasn't happening, but she crawled down to where Tinan lay.

'What is it my lady? Are you having birth pains?' A hand as cold as ice reached out and gripped Takamat.

'I have just shed the waters which will bring our child into the world and now you must help me. The pains are not coming very often, but I think that my time is near.' Takamat knew about birthing as she had helped out with other families, but it was under totally different and safer conditions. Using extreme self control she spoke.

'It would be a good idea if I could look outside to see if the storm has passed and I can then go for help from Mushtari and the other women.'

'That would mean an hour's walk for you, and we both know that your leg would not support that kind of lengthy travel. Stay, I need you here!' Takamat moved past the two dead camels hoping that there might be something on their bodies to help if needed, but when she managed to push the sand with her hands to look outside, it just kept running towards her and piling up at her feet. This was a bad omen. She returned to Tinan.

'The wind is still blowing the sand against the cave opening at the moment. I will have to wait for a little while then have another look to see if I can see daylight.' As it was, the light from the torches had almost been extinguished and she knew that when the cave was in total darkness, Tinan would be in dreadful trouble. She decided to gather around her all the objects that might be useful. There were a few cups and a teapot which must have been used by Nizam, whose dead body was still at the back of the cave. She picked them up and took them over to where the dead camels lay.

Next she carried over the knife which had killed Habib, using it to puncture one of the camel's stomachs so that it released some of the stored water. As this came gushing out she quickly filled the cups and the teapot. The water had a fetid smell, but if it was needed to keep them alive, it would have to do. It was difficult for Takamat to remove the two saddle bags from the camels' heavy bodies, but there was a knife and some dried food which she had packed in readiness for this trip. She hauled the bags to where Tinan lay, hoping that the storm would blow itself out. By now Tinan was in heavy labour. Takamat had grave doubts as to whether she would survive as she seemed to be in some sort of a coma, unable to answer any of the questions put to her. Once again she went to the cave entrance, fiercely digging at the sand which was keeping them prisoners. She couldn't hear the roar of the wind, so hopefully the worst had passed over. Again she dug at the sand until her fingernails bled. She heard Tinan screaming and went immediately to her side, but she had lapsed into semi-consciousness again. This was no good. Takamat knew that the mother had to help to push out the baby, so she summoned up courage and gave her mistress a slap across her face. This worked.

When she opened her eyes, Tinan realized that the pains she felt were heralding the arrival of Habib's child so she gathered a little strength to concentrate on what was happening. Takamat dipped part of the blue turban into the camel water and began to wipe Tinan's face which by now was covered in sweat and sand where she had been lying. This went on for some time, but there were signs that Tinan was growing weary. If she could get some help for the delivery, it might have a better outcome.

When she went to try and move the sand this time she had success. A huge wall of dry sand slid in and covered the two camels' bodies, but there was daylight out there. Feeling more confident and being able to see a lot better, Takamat moved swiftly to Tinan.

'The storm has now passed, so we will soon be out of here. I cannot leave you when you are so close to giving birth, but your family will be on their way to help very soon.'

That help was not forthcoming the 'Simoon' had completely covered the tents of Salaman and his wife and family and most of the town as well. Very few managed to escape the blinding choking sand, but those who did were not aware that Tinan and Takamat were in trouble. The labour was reaching its conclusion, and in a moment of agony, Tinan delivered her baby son. It was stillborn.

Takamat couldn't clean the knife because there was no fire, so she took the dagger from Nizam's body to cut the cord as it was the only one which had not drawn blood. Although not really suitable, she couldn't take any chances with the blood and dirt on the knife which had killed Habib. Turning away from Tinan so that she couldn't see her tears, Takamat wrapped the tiny baby in one of the saddlecloths. She carried it over to where Habib lay, and placed his dead son in his arms.

When she looked again at Tinan she could tell that she also was in trouble because her colour was pasty and her breathing was shallow. Returning to the cups of water, she dipped the cloth into one and wiped Tinan's mouth with it. She reasoned that it wouldn't hurt to tip a little water into her lips, as they seemed so dry. This didn't seem to make any difference so she went to the cave's mouth again for some air, feeling quite helpless.

Takamat frowned then rubbed her eyes. She was looking at a mirage. There was a column of men astride horses, and they were heading towards her. These men had to be Romans as she had seen them in Egypt when she was a young girl. She hadn't forgotten the two Roman guards who had delivered them into the hands of Ben the slave trader. Picking up the brightest piece of saddlecloth, she waved it as she screamed with all her strength. They did not break formation, but the leader must have given the order to move, because they spurred their mounts in response. Two men dismounted and ran towards Takamat, who almost fainted with joy. Quickly she explained that her mistress who had just given birth was in serious need of help from a midwife or healer from the village. After reporting back to their leader, one rode away quickly in that direction. The other came in to attend to Tinan.

His face was a picture of amazement as he found a hacked body outside, and one dead man inside the cave, as well as one dead man with a stillborn baby in his arms and one woman who looked close to death herself. Shortly the rider came back with two people on horses. One was a midwife the other was a healer who knew how to help a woman in this situation. Both of them worked on Tinan, giving her herbs and potions, but it wasn't until they realized that Tinan had not shed the afterbirth that a glimmer of hope appeared. The midwife managed to alleviate this problem by cracking some dried herb in front of Tinan's nostrils which immediately relaxed every muscle in her body releasing the placenta and the fetal membranes. After a while, Tinan's colour returned, but she was still very weak. Takamat took this time to sit down herself and take some fresh water from the soldier. When Tinan finally recognised her friend, she called her over but she didn't say a word about the baby.

The midwife was softly talking to her, telling her to just relax and take things easy until her strength returned, but Tinan knew that there was no baby at her breast, and no sound of its crying either. Asked if she wanted any fresh water to drink, Tinan just shook her head. Takamat asked the two soldiers how they had known where to find them.

'That is another story. We were traveling on this route to the Oasis of Ahaggar when the dust storm hit our legion. We had to ride for our lives, but most of our contingent never made it. What you see here are the only survivors. There were just twenty of us to come out alive. We owe our lives to the common sense and courage of our leader. When we reached this village there were many houses buried beneath the sand. After we rested and watered our horses, a survivor told us that a group of three men with two black slaves had passed through here on their way home after a death in the caves. They were to return with help the next day, but I am sorry to say that this family also became victims of this terrible sandstorm.'

Takamat couldn't believe that all of Salaman's family had perished. Salaman, Mushtari, their two sons and daughers as well as the slaves who had tried to help Habib were all dead. The same fate would have been theirs too if they hadn't been prisoners in this cave. She kept this news to herself, but most of it was overheard by Tinan anyway who showed no evidence of having heard a word. Eventually the soldiers rigged up a portable cot to carry Tinan back to the village where she was made welcome by the healer and his family. When she was carried out, her eyes never found Habib's body. It was as if he never existed. There were no questions, no recriminations and no emotion shown by her. After a week had passed Tinan seemed to be much stronger so she summoned Takamat to her bedside.

'My life here is past, and I am ready to move on now. There is nothing to keep me here, so I intend to ask the Roman leader to give us safe passage to another city. I believe that they are now about to travel to Tombouctou. Tomorrow I want you to arrange a meeting with him, and I will discuss our future plans.'

This was quickly arranged. When they were ushered into his presence, he seemed a little troubled. After taking one look at Tinan the past came flooding back to him. It had to be the girl with the blue eyes, from Egypt. He remembered her friend had a noticeable limp. This couldn't be a co-incidence. Despite her remarkable self assurance, he was still struck by beauty of this young woman. He had been told by one of his men that she had just given birth one week ago to a stillborn babe, but she had ignored it when she left the cave. Marcus was completely at her mercy. Everything which she asked for, he was only too happy to supply. Her friend was not so sure. How could they possibly repay him. They had no money and they were not whores or slaves. Tinan had the answer.

'Although I have silver bangles and a pearl necklace from Mushtari, I will never surrender them. What we do have is something more useful to a man. I will offer him our 'magic fish'. You still have it don't you? It would be of immense assistance when we travel south to Tombouctou. There is still desert to cross and this little fish could prove to be invaluable.'

Takamat silently nodded. Tinan addressed Marcus

'I know that you are agreeable to escorting us to the city of Tombouctou, but because we are not slaves or camp followers, I expect that we will be given every courtesy due to our position.'

Marcus smiled at this impudent young woman who was telling him that she deserved special treatment. The journey would be long and arduous and if water became scarce, they were just two more mouths to share it.

'Just what is your position my lady? I know that you were married to a highly esteemed young man, but surely even a Tuareg is not royalty.'

For a moment Tinan's eyes glowed with intense dislike. He remembered that look so well. It had haunted him for years after he had handed her over to the slavers. She gathered her self control and used a new strength which now came naturally to her and replied.

'For your information the Tuaregs are a noble and highly principled race of people. They are scattered all over the desert, but will always offer support and assistance to anyone in need. They have a culture which is strong with links from one side of this country to the other. They choose to live their own lives in freedom but they live by rules of right and wrong, and unlike the Roman Empire, do not seek to convert other races to their religion.'

'Just a minute young lady, those are dangerous words. Do not let anyone else hear you speak like that again. As to your payment for your journey, you will be my guests as I feel that I owe you both a debt anyway.'

Tinan had no idea what he meant, but she felt assured by his comments and said to him with a winning smile, as she placed the small pouch into his hand.

'Sir, I would like to offer you the only thing of value that I have in my possession.' He opened it, expecting to find a precious stone or a gold coin, but was a little disappointed to find a small silver fish inside a clear cylinder which wobbled and seemed to point away from him. As he turned it around it still seemed to point in only one direction.

'This fish is made from a magnetic property called lodestone and will always point towards the North Star. This means that wherever you are going, it will always pinpoint the direction in which you wish to journey. I would like to give it to you as a token of my trust and appreciation for your kind hospitality.' Marcus took the object, returned it to the purse and handed it back to her.

'I thank you for this kind offer but I have no where to store it, so I suggest that you wear it for me.

If at any time we need this, I will know where to find it.'

The column moved out the next day, south through the desert and onto the caravan trade routes. Tinan was just twenty years old. Weeks passed slowly. The two women had been given horses to ride, and once again this was a little harrowing for Tinan, but she was determined that a new life awaited her and nothing was going to prevent her pursuit of it. Marcus paid little attention to her, except to occasionally ask about her health and comfort. He showed no special interest in her so she was perhaps a little disappointed. She felt that when they had spoken alone, he seemed to project a certain curiosity in her.

The city of Tombouctou was reached at last. Everyone was glad to dismount to find lodgings with a bath and decent food. Marcus was given accommodation in the barracks, but he firstly made sure that Tinan and Takamat were housed in a local Inn, where he gave the proprietors a few coins for their trouble. They were very happy to have such ladies of quality staying with them. Situated at the crossroads of a trade route, Tombouctou drew people from all over the country. The markets there were unrivalled displaying such wares as gold, salt, spices and slaves. This city became a mecca for the meeting of intelligent minds searching for enlightenment. Shopping regularly became a pleasure for Takamat.

The excitement of the marketplace was one incentive where she listened to the gossip, but she became aware that the standard of conversation was far superior to anything that she had encountered. She returned to her mistress that afternoon and told her.

'I have stopped in the streets and listened to the men drinking tea at small tables and they talk about all sorts of wondrous things. There is such a thing they call medicine which seems a little like our herbs and salves, and there are buildings which are so large that they could house a thousand people. I have heard also talk of a gold mine which contains endless wealth, and of new techniques to control and produce crops of great plenty.'

This information ignited Tinan's appetite for such learning. This was to be her new focus. Women were not considered inferior in this city but she would have to enlist some help if she wanted to gain some of this wonderful knowledge. She made an appointment to see the garrison Commander. Marcus was more than pleased to see her, but he was not expecting to hear her request.

'It has come to my attention that there are many wonderful things to learn in this city, and I want you to help me influence some of these teachers so that I can attend their classes.' He had to hide a smile.

'But women don't attend them. The scholars are all men.'

'That may be the case, but I have noticed that they mostly cover their faces with a turban, so I intend to do the same. I will borrow some suitable masculine clothes to disguise myself and will cover my face too.' Marcus couldn't help himself as he laughed at her audacity, but he could see that expression of determination and he recognised it all too well. As the Garrison Commander he did have great authority in this city, so he used it. He wasn't really surprised when the accolades came to his notice about 'that young man,' and his ability to acquire knowledge at an extremely high level. This continued for two years. Tinan had found a fountain of interest, study and learning, which filled her every waking hour.

Marcus tried to interest her in riding with him in the desert, but she would have none of it. She suspected that he had other motives and she was not interested in encouraging him down a path that led nowhere. There was one exception. He was holding a thirtieth birthday party, so he invited Tinan and Takamat to attend. Takamat in all innocence asked him if he wanted them to sing for him. He certainly did, but she would have to persuade her mistress on that score. To make it sweeter, he assured Takamat that his guests would include some of the finest teachers in Tombuoctou. Her mistress was not interested in going to this party until Takamat dangled the bait about the party guests. This changed everything, because although Tinan had only met them as a disguised 'young man,' she longed to be able to hold a discourse with these men at a different level. She consented after some deliberation. Although she had never considered how Takamat managed to buy food and clothing, Tinan expected that their 'protector,' was responsible. So when she was presented with a glorious new gown for the occasion she took it as something which she deserved anyway.

Takamat had been told by Marcus that Tinan was to have anything that she wanted, as he would be more than happy to pay the cost. She knew that it was more than likely that he was in love with Tinan, but it was unlikely to be returned. Nevertheless, it was time that Tinan knew the score and didn't take everything for granted. They had both lived on his generosity for long enough. She was going to have a talk to Tinan about that, but she couldn't help feel that there was something familiar about Marcus. As she helped Tinan into this stunning cream silk full length dress, she admired the off one shoulder design which Tinan topped with her lovely pearl necklace.

'There is one condition that we have to fulfill tonight and that is to entertain his guests with a song. Marcus has asked me to find suitable women to accompany us on the harp and flutes. I will play the castanets whilst you sing.'

'What do you mean? I thought that we were his guests. I haven't done this for years, and it is certainly short notice.'

For once in her life Takamat decided to strongly disagree with her mistress as she spoke in a firm voice.

'Who do you think has looked after us for the past two years, providing you with every comfort, including the beautiful dress which you are wearing? He has been more than generous and it is his birthday after all. If you can't see how badly you're behaving, then I feel ashamed for you.' With her mouth open to say something, Tinan couldn't find the words, but she did manage to nod her head, and smile.

When Marcus came to the door to collect them, he looked so handsome in his full dress uniform. Takamat looked at him with unabashed approval. This time he was lost for words as he took in the vision of loveliness which greeted him. Tinan was resplendent in the gown he had bought for her. Tonight she had woven little strings of beads through her dark hair which was piled up high in a Roman style to match her dress. She was given the place of honour next to him and he enjoyed hearing all the comments about this mysterious foreign woman.

Of course he would not disclose who she was or where she came from, but his proud smile was evident to all. After the meal had been cleared away,

Marcus announced that this lady and her maidservant would honour them with a song sung in the Egyptian language. There were more murmurs about her background. Was she perhaps an Egyptian princess?

Takamat took her place next to Tinan with the other women who played the harp, flutes, castanets, and drums. Beautiful music filled the room. Marcus was entranced, and so were his guests. They begged for more, so this time Tinan played the harp herself, Takamat joined her, as they sang a love song from their days in the desert. It was nothing like the ones which she had sung for Habib, but both women knew it well and sang it in that language. Tinan's voice was strong with the emotion of a lost love which is exactly what she had known, but although her eyes grew misty, she didn't shed a tear. Once again there was great enthusiasm from the seated guests, and when she returned to the table, Tinan was rushed with questions.

'Do you speak both the Egyptian and the Arabic language? Was that song sung in a Bedouin dialect? Can you help us to learn these other tongues?'

On it went until Tinan grew weary of these countless enquiries. She had wanted to have discussions with some of these men, but not about music or language. If they were that interested, perhaps everyone could acquire what they wanted. When the evening ended Marcus took both women home, but Takamat left them at the door, saying that she had a headache. She thanked him and retired. He said to Tinan.

'You were wonderful tonight and all my instincts about you proved to be correct.'

'Thank you Marcus,' (This was the first time that she had addressed him by his name), but I think that it is I who should be acknowledging all that you have done for us. I have accepted your protection and your generosity without giving you my thanks. I can only apologise for my churlish behaviour. I wonder why you have tolerated it for so long.'

'You really don't remember do you? When you were a young girl in Pharaoh's temple and you were taken and sold into slavery, I was one of the guards who had the unpleasant job of doing that. That is why I will always be happy to support and assist your move into the world of learning. Perhaps after tonight you will not be in need of my help. All the learned men were fascinated by your charming knowledge of language and music. I am sure that their wives, though perhaps a little jealous will rush to invite you to attend their social gatherings.'

She stared at him as if she was seeing him for the first time. So much had happened since that day, and here he was in her life at a time when all she wanted to do was to immerse her intellectual capacity in the halls of knowledge and wisdom. As she was silent, Marcus bent towards her and gently took her into his arms. She knew that he was going to kiss her and she wasn't disappointed. Tinan felt her body swaying towards his, enjoying what she was feeling, but she quickly pulled away.

'You are right about my quest for knowledge. That is all I'm interested in. I appreciate what you have done tonight and in the past, but you don't owe me anything and shouldn't feel that you had to make it up to me. I am on a pathway which was meant to be. I shall continue on it for as long as I possibly can.'

Marcus had been told in the most pleasant manner that Tinan's life did not revolve around his and as much as he had hoped differently, he accepted it. When he kissed her, he felt that she was returning his approach to a possible amorous relationship, but now he knew that was not the case. When she let herself into the house, she went straight to see if Takamat was still awake.

'Takamat tonight was wonderful despite my misgivings. I really enjoyed meeting with the local scholars and teachers. What shocked me was the fact that Marcus told me that he was responsible for taking us to the slave traders all those years ago. Everything fell into place when he said that, but I told him to forget any obligation to us, as we're happy with our lives.'

'I should've known that there was something familiar about him. He was just a young man then, but he has grown into a handsome and virile leader.

How do you feel about him now? I'm sure that he has strong feelings for you. I have watched his face light up whenever he sees you, and you must be aware of it too.'

'I have a deep regard for him because he is our protector and confidante, but he knows how I feel about the future. I will always welcome him as a friend.'

Takamat smiled at this comment and shook her head. Marcus was more than a friend. He would attempt to be a suitor whether Tinan accepted this fact or not. She sleepily said goodnight.

After the success of Marcus's birthday party, Tinan became well known in Tombouctou. She was encouraged to give lessons in the Egyptian language. The same was true of the Arabic and Tuareg dialects. She now entered the seats of learning as herself. (The young man had disappeared). Tinan gave all her energies to acquiring expertise on agriculture, the seasons, the harvesting of water through ditches from a water source, growing of crops and various other methods of ensuring a ready food supply.

She also studied some methods used to help with illness and injuries as well as using hygiene in these applications. There were discussions about the heavens and the stars, a little of which Tinan knew about. She certainly knew the relevance of the North Star.

Her favourite subject became the learning of mathematics. She was fascinated about the numbers and their importance in everyday life, especially in business dealings. Added to this she admired the beautiful geometric lines which were used to decorate and define silver jewelry.

Because of her standing in the community, she was visited by Tuareg craftsmen who knew of her efforts to improve her own life and hopefully the lives of her people. They showed her the ways in which their life story could be engraved onto silver, and they encouraged her to allow them to do the same for her. She was captivated by the lovely pieces and also the inclusion of the alphabet which was an artistic joy in itself. Deciding to take this step she commissioned a craftsman to make up two silver bracelets: one for herself and one for Takamat. The size differed because Takamat was of a smaller build with a smaller wrist, but apart from that they had to be identical.

The artist was overjoyed to be able to make this for this lady whom he considered was a Tuareg Queen. That is where the seed germinated about Tinan. When he enquired about the design, Tinan advised that she would provide that herself. He was surprised at her drawing which seemed to represent a mountain range with high hills and low valleys, but she knew perfectly well that range with those caves which were forever imprinted in her memory.

Marcus had taken to riding in the hills around Tombouctou and Tinan now joined him regularly. When they stopped for some refreshment, Marcus asked her about her studies and how would she use it in the future. She didn't hesitate as she knew exactly how.

'My life has been full of pain and heartache until I came here and found the light of wisdom. Now I want to gather these shining lights and use them to make a better existence for my people. I am going to build a city.'

He did not laugh or reproach her, because in five years this woman had blossomed before his eyes. She was popular, clever, sympathetic and wise and he knew that she could do anything if she put her mind to it.

'You are going to need more than artisans and builders to do this my dear lady. Have you thought about the cost of all this? It would be far beyond anything which you and I have to spend.'

'Yes Marcus I have. I propose to hold a sporting event, the like of which has never been seen in this land. As you know the Bedouins and the Tuaregs are fiercely proud of their riding skills and some are also incredible archers. This event will be in the form of competitions between men with their wonderful horses, camel races, games as well as similar contests. There will be a small token as an entrance fee, which will help to provide a purse to the winners, but the main idea is to get these families together at the one meeting place and to hold this gathering every year at the same time on the same day.'

'But when will that day be? How can you hope to get so many people to know when this gathering will take place?'

'That is the easy part. At the end of summer after harvest time is the week when this will take place. These nomads live in tents anyway, so it is no problem for them to roll them up and make it here for this special celebration. Apart from the events which I have mentioned there will be music and good food to enjoy. You might not believe it to be so, but my people are a proud race, loyal to their land, but happiest when they're entertaining guests and relatives. They are very sociable'

'You seem to have thought of everything but there could be strong rivalry and resentment if tempers are frayed. What then?'

'That is when you come into it. I would expect that a few guards from your garrison would only be too happy to oversee this special occasion.'

'I can see that you are serious about this. I will make sure that the word is spread far and wide. Let me know the details when you can, but I fear that this will still take many years to fill the coffers to build your city.'

'You are quite right Marcus, but the other reason for doing this is to show the Tuaregs who seem to shun the cities, that they can still retain their love of the open spaces, whilst at the same time, move to a more advanced stage of social development by visiting the other side of human relations in a different arena, such as a city.'

'I think that it is time for us to return, but before we do that, I want to ask you if you have changed your mind about me. I am your shield and will always put your interests before mine, but I love you Tinan and I would like to make you my wife.'

'This is not the time for us to be talking about marriage.

I have told you about my plans and dreams for the future, so please give me some time to put them into action. I value your friendship and all that you have done for me over the years, but marriage is like a slave bracelet tethered to my ankle and I am not that sort of woman anymore.'

They rode back in relative silence, as Tinan knew that he must be disappointed with her answer to his proposal, but she gave him her honest views about everything. He was the only male companion that she had, but she did not need a lover. When Marcus left her new apartment, she went inside to tell Takamat about her ideas for a sporting event for all the clans. She found her sitting in the front room with a young man. She guessed by his dress and speech that he was a local inhabitant of Tombouctou, but he seemed friendly and pleasant enough to cause Takamat's face to shine. Later when she asked about him Takamat was pleased to talk about him with glowing details.

They had met in the market place, where she had tripped over a clay pot from his stall. He felt obliged to help her home and had stayed for a little while to talk. This led to his request to come again and visit with her. She agreed. Tinan was so happy for her friend because up until now there had not been a man who showed the slightest interest in Takamat. It didn't take long before they became betrothed. Tinan was so pleased that happiness was to be given to someone who so richly deserved it. Takamat was still a young woman but she had given up hope that she would ever marry. Her slight affliction didn't seem to worry Ahmed, and he thought that she was both beautiful and clever. Their wedding was simple and special. Ahmed was not a wealthy man, but he had a large family who prepared a wedding feast filled with love and laughter. Takamat moved in with his family until they could find a place of their own, working with him on his clay pot stall at the market.

She was amused to think that her lameness which caused her to trip over a clay pot had been the reason which brought her happiness.

Tinan found plenty to do to fill in her daylight hours, as her studies kept her occupied, but after Takamat's move she now knew loneliness too. She decided that it would be a good idea if she began to entertain some of the local inhabitants. Social gatherings were good for everyone. With Marcus who was a wonderful host at her side, she could assure a dinner with good conversation and humorous stories. She planned to ask him this week when they had their usual ride. Marcus cancelled this outing, telling her that he had another invitation to visit one of his men and his new bride.

She accepted this but went riding anyway to the usual place in the hills outside the city. This was one of the few times when she was really alone, but that thought didn't cross her mind. When some small animal ran across the path in front of her horse, spooking him and causing him to rear, she fell heavily. Her horse took off and cantered back to the stables. When she tried to get up, she winced as her ankle seemed to be giving her intense pain. She thought to herself.

'This will not do at all. I can't walk back in this condition, but when my horse arrives without me, someone at the stables will raise the alarm and come for me.' She managed to drag herself to a large rock and perched herself on it to wait. Then something strange happened: it began to rain. This was in itself an unusual event at this time of year. Tinan scowled at the sky, as the rain was spoiling her clothing and her hair was becoming a bedraggled mess. She managed to hobble over to the mouth of a nearby cave.

'Not again,' she thought. 'My whole life has been filled with time spent in caves when I didn't want to be there.'

Her bright red scarf was left at the cave's entrance to indicate her position. After a while she began to look around her and was surprised to see some sort of light coming from the back of the cave.

'That is strange,' she thought. 'I have never seen anything like that before.' As she moved towards it she gave a little cry because her ankle was beginning to swell and she thought that perhaps it was broken. Now she was feeling miserable. As she began to shiver, her eyes rested on something which was small and shining brightly with a yellow glow. Running her finger over it, it seemed cold and hard. Could it possibly be gold? She thought about her scarf, dragged herself back to where it lay on the ground, and placed it on a rock. The rain still continued with the sky turning an angry grey colour. Now she was annoyed because someone should have come looking for her by now. The rain was kicking up mud onto her clothes, so she moved to the back of the cave where she found a place to keep dry. She was asleep when Marcus found her.

It had taken some time before the stable hand had found him. He mounted his horse and went looking for her. Having some idea as to where she may have gone, he rode out to find her, hoping that she had found some shelter from the rain. His vision was not good at this time, so he turned his horse around intending to return, but then he saw a red puddle lying on a rock. This turned out to be her red scarf, so he alighted from his horse and tied the reins to a tree. When he saw Tinan, his heart jumped because she looked so pale and defenceless in a state which she rarely exhibited. He bent over her, took hold of her shoulders and kissed her. Tinan's eyes flew open as she realized that Marcus had at last found her. She moved to get up but again the sharp pain in her ankle affected her balance.

'Marcus, I have been stupid in riding out here alone and now look at what I've done. I think that I have twisted my ankle and I have interrupted your visit with your friends. I am sorry.'

He wasn't able to think very straight at this stage because his desire for her got the better of him. Marcus had been a very patient man. With contained emotion he spoke to her.

'My visit was not as important as my concern for you. It would be futile to leave here now because it is dark and the rain is still falling heavily. I didn't think to bring a dry change of clothes for you, but I am sure that we can stay the night here in relative comfort.'

Tinan began to shiver as the cold began to creep through her wet clothes. Marcus noticed this and once again held her body against his to try to warm her. She didn't resist. Tinan allowed him to remove her wet outer garments and spread them out to dry on a rock. Turning back to her he took her into his arms again. After a while his warmth stopped her from shivering, but Marcus was more than aroused as his hand found her breast with its raised hard nipple. It had been years since Tinan had felt the fire rip through her belly, but as Marcus awoke her passion, she knew that she needed him tonight as much as he needed her. Earlier he had turned his riding cloak inside out and placed it on the ground. He gently lowered Tinan onto it.

Despite her painful ankle, she welcomed his embrace and the love which she had long denied this man. He was not Habib, and she felt a sting of remorse about accepting Marcus in this way, but this was here and now. Habib had been her true love and nothing would ever change that, but that seemed so long ago. The night had closed in, but by now the rain had stopped and the stars were out. Marcus could not keep his ardour for too long because he had waited years for this moment to arrive. His love for her had been kept confined but now he hoped that she would return his affection with the same intensity.

Before dawn they made love again but this time it was with greater emotion and Marcus took his time to please her until she cried out with ecstasy. Tinan could hardly believe that she felt this happy and satisfied. It wasn't that she had forgotten how it felt, but she had to admit that her physical needs had been locked away. Today her body's warmth spread tingling sensations which seemed to pervade every part of her. When Marcus felt that they should be on their way, he gave her the dried clothes and helped to dress her. Her ankle seemed to be a little better and she stood ready to leave with him.

'Last night was very special for me, and completely unexpected, but we had better return before someone sends out a party to look for us. There might be some very awkward questions to answer.' They both returned on his horse with little conversation. On reaching her apartment Marcus spoke seriously.

'My beautiful lady, you must know how long I have loved you. The time has come for you to make a decision. I am asking you to come and live with me as my wife. Your days of study and learning must be coming to a close so we can have a wonderful life together. I am aware of your plans to hold sporting competitions and I think that this will be a great way to introduce the binding of the clans. However, we could do this together as an indivisible team as man and wife, to enforce their credibility with an official confirmation.' Tinan was tempted to take this path, but something was not right and she didn't know what it was.

'Marcus, you have honoured me with your proposal. I am aware of your hopes for our future, but I have always been honest with you, so I have to express my true feelings. I can never love you in the same way that you love me, and because of this it would be unfair to tie you to such an arrangement. If you still feel the same way at the end of summer which is only a few months away, I shall give you my answer at the gathering on the first day of that week. This gives us both some time to think about it. In the meantime, this will be the first of hopefully such yearly events and I have much to prepare.'

Marcus was disappointed, but he had waited for years to possess her, so a few months more would not be unreasonable he told himself.

'You have always held my heart and my future in your hands, so I will wait for you till then. As you are still a little indisposed I will send a female slave here to attend you until you are better. I haven't discussed your plans for the gathering but I am happy to tell you that there has been much interest shown by the local men of many faiths and cultures, as well as those who have heard about it from the caravan traders. You will be pleasantly surprised when they start to arrive here.'

When she had recovered from her sprained ankle, she paid a visit to Takamat who was busy and happy in her new life.

'Takamat, I am so pleased that you have found contentment and that your business is also keeping you well occupied. I have received this week a lovely gift from a local silversmith of two silver bracelets which I asked him to make. They are identical except that yours is smaller to fit your little wrist. Here it is.'

'Oh it is lovely with such an unusual pattern all over it. Did you design it?'

'Yes I did. We have both shared many experiences together, some not so good, but you have saved my life more than once. These bracelets are reminders of my love and appreciation for all that you have done for me. I designed the outer edge as a profile of the mountains of Ahaggar where I will return one day to build a city for my people. The other news is that Marcus has asked me to marry him. I have promised to give him my answer at the gathering of the clans after harvest. When that happens, I will accept Marcus if he still wants me. When I move to his house, I would like you and Ahmed to have my apartment.'

'That is very generous of you, but what is the 'gathering of the clans'?

'I was going to tell you the night that I first met Ahmed, but you both were so happy and had your own wedding to plans, that I wanted to wait. Marcus and I have planned to gather the Bedouin and Tuareg tribes for a week's competition after the end of summer's harvest. There will be horse racing, camel races and other games. There will also be a small entry fee which will go towards the winner's purse in these contests. There already has been interest shown by the locals and Marcus tells me that the same has been received by the caravan traders who have spread the word on their travels.'

'That sounds wonderful. Will there be food for sale too?'

'Yes Takamat, you and Ahmed could take charge of moving the market there by spreading the word here. A small fee would be charged to each stallholder. If this becomes a successful undertaking, it will be held each year at the same time, and the profit made from the day will be held until we return to Ahaggar to build a city.'

'This seems such a wonderful idea. You truly have found a way to bring the clans together at one place where they can socialize and perhaps learn a thing or two. I thank you for this lovely bracelet, and I wish you every success in this upcoming gathering.'

When she next saw Marcus, Tinan told him that she had something to tell him that could be of great importance.

'I forgot to mention something interesting that I found in the cave where you found me'.

'Under the circumstances I am not surprised. You were in pain until we found something to make you forget it.'

'That is not how it happened, or how I recall it. I wasn't expecting that I would feel that way about you, and you know just how much my desire for you matched your own,' she flashed.

'Yes Tinan, it seems almost like a dream to me, but what else did you want to tell me?'

'I have never seen gold except when it has been turned into coins or jewelry but that day in that cave I saw something which looked very much like it. It was in a seam or line and had a wonderful yellow colour. When we left there, I was not thinking about anything else except you.'

'Perhaps we had better ride out and have a look at this.'

Returning to the cave, he crawled to the back where she indicated. Marcus was astonished at the size of the seam. It was wide and long, travelling onwards through the rock. There seemed to be another layer starting beneath the end line too. He considered the serious consequences of this find.

'We will have to get an expert to confirm that this is what I think it is, but of greater importance we must also establish the ownership of this land. I do not want any knowledge of this to get out, so it will be better if we don't say a word to anyone. I will go immediately to the local authorities and enquire about it, and if it doesn't belong to anyone I will buy it, on the proviso that I can pay within the month.'

Marcus could hardly believe his luck. The rocky and useless land belonged to a local family, who had bequeathed this to Ahmed and Takamat as a wedding present. That night he took Tinan to visit them telling them that he had a proposition to put before them.

After the tea had been served with some flat bread, the two women retired to sit in the background. Marcus began.

'I believe that you own some land in the surrounding hills which I am asking you to sell to me. Before you ask me why I want it, I will tell you that perhaps it has gold in it. I am prepared to pay you for the land as well as pay for the necessary mining tools needed, if you agree. I also propose that we draw up a legal agreement because it will take some money to fund its extraction. If you don't want to include Tinan and myself, and prefer to dig it out yourself, I will understand. As yet I have not had an assessor confirm that it is gold, but that will take place when you give us your answer. This could be a wonderful chance for all of us to accumulate wealth, but please think about it and be discreet about the discussion.'

Ahmed waited for Marcus to finish speaking, then he said.

'This sounds as if it could be the answers to all our prayers, and I agree about the necessity of keeping quiet about the possibility of the importance of your find. Please be assured that we will talk about your possible discovery and will contact you very soon.'

When they had left, Ahmed turned to his wife and smiled.

'This seems unbelievable. I am not a rich man so I could never hope to pay for the mine to be worked.

We could tell my family about it and hope that they could lend us the money to do that, or we could accept Marcus's offer to pay for the land and the mining. This would still give us a wonderful income if it turns out to be a gold mine. What do you think about it?'

'I am still in a state after listening to what Marcus had to say. If your land covers a large area we could search for ever and not find the mine. That is if you decide to try to do this alone, or with your family.

If you trust him to handle it for you, there would be little need for you to outlay any cash to get it all started.'

'Firstly, this is our land, not just mine. It was a wedding gift from my parents. Secondly you have known Marcus and Tinan for many years and I am sure that you trust them to be honest in their dealings. After all he is the Garrison Commander. I know that Tinan is held in high regard by the citizens of this city. You are quite right about our lack of funds to contribute to the workings. I very much doubt whether my family would have anything near what will be needed to begin. Even if we used the money from the sale of our land to Marcus, there would be many questions asked as to why he would want to buy worthless land.

If we agree to his proposal after he has had the lode confirmed it might put him into a dangerous position if this find becomes common knowledge. If we agree to sell the land first, with a condition that any workings are to be equally shared, it should be all legally settled without too much detail involved, but you and I know that any guess about this would spread like wildfire.'

'I agree with your thinking Ahmed, but once this document has been made legal it still could be dangerous for us all.

I do believe that Marcus would send some of his men to guard the entrance but when it becomes operational, there would be a need for strict security.'

'So are we agreed to sell the land to our friends and form a partnership?'

'From my part, I am saying yes,' replied Takamat.

When Ahmed and Takamat agreed to Marcus's proposal it proved to be an incredible source of wealth for them. A small sample taken to the Assessor was confirmed as genuine, so work began under strict supervision with much excitement from all involved. The land which contained these deposits was sizeable. It had to be fenced off from any would be intruders doing a little bit of private digging. As time went by, Marcus investigated the possibility of the gold seams running under and into other cave seams. He was successful in locating these, but now seemed to be spending most of his time at the site. (This meant that he had to delegate other officers to take his place at the garrison, a move which didn't please everyone).

The same was true for Ahmed and Takamat. The market stall had been handed over to a family member so this situation freed up the couple to work in this area when they needed to relieve Marcus.

The weeks were fast approaching when Tinan expected her gathering to begin. She asked Marcus to ride with her to the cleared area where it was to be held, so that they could design the layout. It was very likely to be dusty when all this took place so they agreed that the food stalls and tents should be situated quite a distance from the competitors. As they finished their inspection Marcus told Tinan.

'I have heard from Rome and it is possible that I may be replaced. Apparently there have been some complaints from certain quarters of the community suggesting that I have been spending too much time at the mine. If that happens I shall resign my commission. We are becoming so wealthy that it might be better if I do. I may have to take a more committed role with the management of the mining anyway. If this continues to be as profitable as it has been, it could be possible that we can begin to build that city of yours.'

Tinan knew that the moment was fast approaching when she would have to make her decision to accept Marcus and his proposal of marriage. She had promised to give him her answer on the first day of the Clan gathering, which was due within a few weeks. Knowing that her work here was almost at an end, she couldn't think of any other living man with whom she would want to share this project. All through the week, preparations had been put in place for the competitions, with families arriving from many destinations.

Marcus had sent some of his men to facilitate the erecting of the tents and the competition sites were clearly marked and ready to go.

Takamat had also been busy with the market stall holders who were quite excited about the prospect of good business and the meeting of new people. She had another reason to be excited. She was pregnant.

Today was the opening day of the gathering. Marcus called for Tinan wearing his full dress uniform with a confident smile. She was dressed as a Tuareg lady of high rank in a blue long dress with a grey and silver jacket. She covered her long dark hair with a matching shawl. This was complemented by exquisite silver ear-rings, bracelets and a stunning silver necklace. She carried a silver and peacock feather fan. When they arrived astride two magnificent horses, there was an uproar, as some of the tribes came rushing to see this beautiful woman and her handsome companion. Tinan deliberately did not request a fanfare or even any troops to accompany her there. She didn't want these people to see her as anything other than a noble lady who did not need protection or the pomp and intimidation from a Roman contingent.

On a specially raised dais she sat beside Marcus and enjoyed the incredible spectacle. No artist could have captured the colour, excitement and amazement seen on that first day. On every stall and on every corner there were banners flying. The women were dressed in their brightest clothing, and despite having to ride and compete, the men were dressed in their best clothes. The sound of music with drums and pipes was constantly heard, only adding to the frenzy. The horses were obviously affected and became skittish and hard to control. One took off racing at great speed with its colourful saddlecloth flapping around its legs. This only served to spur it on to run faster. Marcus spoke to Tinan with something close to humour saying.

'That is one horse which has no chance of winning. It will wear itself out before the race has begun.' Tinan's memory took her back to another race, another time when a young man had hoped for her hand but he had been outsmarted by Omar. That seemed a lifetime away.

All day the wonderful aromas of food could be detected coming from the many tents circling this festive celebration. Although, there were no speeches given, the enthusiasm of those attending was palpable. Many came just to see her, and before the day had ended, a chant was heard from the crowd around her. 'Tinan Hinan,'our Queen. Tinan Hinan our Queen.' Marcus knew that he would hear this intonation some day. He had also found the same message in the city as she was now considered to be Royalty. He recognised the importance of what was happening and decided to speak to the crowd.

'We are pleased that today has turned out to be a day to remember for all of us. Tinan Hinan is responsible for this and she organized this day so that you could enjoy your culture, interaction with sporting events and the coming together of the many tribes of the desert. This is more than just a friendly gathering, it is a mark of respect for each other and hopefully a closer tie to the appreciation of your heritage.'

Once more there were cheers and chanting of Tinan Hinan our Queen. Tinan sat with a serious expression as she knew that after today things would never be quite the same. She had wanted to bring her people together for their enjoyment of their love of sport, but even more so because they were scattered all over the desert. They needed to be aware that they were a united race in many ways. She didn't expect the adoration or the passionate affirmation of the public declaration, but obviously Marcus did. When the day ended he took her hand. Without a word, his eyes asked the question which Tinan had promised to answer on this day.

'Marcus this day has been beyond my expectations. I have to accept the fact that once again I owe you my appreciation for all that transpired.

Apart from your heartfelt speech which echoed my feelings, you also bound the clans into a united people, who have now chosen me for their Queen. I am not of royal blood, a fact which you once pointed out, but I feel in every fibre of my body and heart that I will become their Queen. If this has been written in the stars and comes to pass, I want you beside me every step of the way, so my answer to your question is Yes.'

'I always knew that I was meant to be your husband because when I first gazed into your lovely blue eyes many years ago, I saw my future in them. Something galvanized my heart which has always belonged to you. The fact that it took years of us both wandering in the desert in different directions also was meant to be, because when we finally met I knew that the fates had shone kindly on me at last. As far as the tribes acknowledging your place and status, don't dismiss your elevated standing. Despite the fact that you told me about being found in a basket floating on the Nile you could have been the result of an unwanted baby from a person of high birth. Blue eyes were rarely seen in Egypt, except in some of the Roman forces or visiting Emperors. Your carriage and bearing confirms this.'

'I will never know my origins, but whatever has happened in my past has truly prepared me for what is about to take place in my future. I am ready now to move to the Ahaggar Mountains and begin to construct what has been my long held dream. After you have announced our betrothal, I shall inform the builders, scholars and other enlightened persons that we are looking for the finest artisans and craftsmen to join us in the building of a new life in a new city.'

He heard all that he needed to confirm that Tinan would become his wife. Marcus knew that their new life together would be a beginning of something extraordinary. Despite whatever problems arose, her passionate interest in the future would keep her active, focused and happy. He would be by her side to share that journey with her.

'Have you thought about the time and place for our Wedding Day? I will be resigning my position with the Legion and will need to attend to our business interests before we are ready to start our move north.'

'Yes I have given it much thought. I have decided that our Wedding will take place when we arrive at Abalessa in the mountains. I wish to have as many of the tribes as possible attending. As this will take some time to arrange we can start sending out this invitation as soon as possible. Today is only the first day at the gathering but I would like our coming nuptials to be announced there. In that way, they can move to Abalessa at the conclusion of the games, enjoying our hospitality and celebrations. To move there with their tents and households would not be too difficult because the harvest time is over. A little time spent away from their ancestral lands would not be much of a problem, and perhaps some may like to permanently join us in Abalessa.'

He smiled again at her incredible capacity for forward thinking. If these days were anything to go by, Tinan was going to make a marvelous Tuareg Queen. That night he arranged a moonlit dinner for them both. She had not moved in with him yet, so he called for her at her apartment with a surprise. When she opened the door, a man stood there dressed in flowing robes and wearing a blue turban which covered most of his face. Tinan's heart skipped a beat. He looked so dashing dressed in the local garb that she really wasn't sure. He was as tall as Marcus and he certainly had his eyes.

'Is that you Marcus? I really didn't expect you to dress like this, but you look wonderful!'

Thank you, my beloved. I thought that as I am to become the consort to a Queen, I had better start looking like one. I have asked my servants to prepare and leave a meal for us. So if you are ready we can go.' The night was soft and starry with just a gentle breeze which stirred Tinan's hair. She covered it with a transparent scarf with little pearls which dropped against her forehead. This time she wore the finest dress of pale green silk which had come from the Orient. As usual her arm was adorned with silver bracelets, and she looked every inch a Royal Queen. A table was set on a balcony with the best cheese, fruit, and wine together with a classical Bedouin dish called a fetir or sweet pancake. He had ordered this light meal because tonight he intended that everything should be perfect. Tinan could tell by the expression in his eyes that Marcus had more than just a meal on his mind, so she became a little adventurous herself. Perhaps the wine helped her but she decided to play a game with him. As each course ended she asked him to remove one layer of his clothes. He did this without question, but his eyes opened wide when she decided to do the same.

After the last glass of wine she stood naked. Her long hair was blowing around her shoulders playing hide and seek across her beautiful breasts. Marcus stood there transfixed. By this time he also was down to his bare underclothing so he took her hand and led her to the bedroom. This room was small and richly decorated. He had used some aromatic herbs: myrrh, frankincense and mint which were placed in small pots around the room. Wanting tonight to be memorable for them both, he surprised her by leading her into another small room where a perfumed bathtub, surrounded by candles stood on a tiled floor. He stepped into it and asked her to join him. When she did this he removed his own underclothing and lowered himself into the warm bath pulling her body towards him. She smiled as she realized that the only place for her to sit was over his erect penis which he slowly sank into her. She placed her hands around his neck as he watched her eyes when she felt him enter her. This was a perfect ending to what Marcus had planned for a long time. Now she was truly his and he knew that he loved her more than anything else in his world. Tinan was happy and enjoyed their lovemaking which continued out of the bath then onto the bed. After many hours they both fell asleep exhausted.

He accepted that Tinan wanted to get her project started and that they would wed as soon as they reached Abalessa so the next day he put all their shared plans into practise. The announcement made at the gathering was received with wild delight. Their Tuareg Queen was getting married in the Ahaggar Mountains. Everyone was invited to make the trip. Marcus had informed his ex-brothers in arms as well as the local townsfolk. The news spread like wildfire as both of these persons were held in high regard by the poor and rich alike in the city. The invitation was given to those who wanted a new life to join the wedding celebrations, then to stay on and help build a new city.

Tinan had forgotten one very important fact. This was that her friend Takamat had not been informed about the latest developments. When she received a visit from her friend she realized this oversight was a damaging one which she could have avoided. Takamat had heard the news of their betrothal, and the fact that Tinan was now living with

Marcus, but she had not seen or spoken to Tinan personally. Takamat was ushered into her presence by a servant. When she saw who it was, Tinan warmly embraced her friend, but was surprised to note a different expression on her face.

'Welcome my dear friend. It seems so long since we have shared any time together. The fault is mine and I must apologise to you for that. As you know the gathering of the tribes has been hugely successful, and after that Marcus and I announced our betrothal. We have not even celebrated it with any special dinner for our friends as we have so much to organise before we move from Tombouctou.'

'I congratulate you both on that wonderful news and I do understand that you have been busy, but so have we. Not only is Ahmed constantly at work overseeing the mine, but we are going to have an addition to our family. I am pregnant.' Tinan clapped her hands with joy.

'That is indeed special news. I can only say that I am so happy for you both. I shall ask Marcus to visit you to talk about the future and the exciting prospects for us all'.

After Takamat left Tinan felt despondent. She had failed to include her best friend in the news of her coming wedding and then to hear the announcement of Takamat's pregnancy sent shivers of remorse through her. In all the years, the subject of her own lost child had never been raised but now she felt the loss keenly. As much as she loved Takamat this was something which she would feel with envy, watching her belly swell during the coming months. Tinan discussed with Marcus, her friend's visit as well as the fact that she felt badly for having neglected her. Could they make a visit soon to correct this situation? Marcus didn't see this concern very often in Tinan, but he knew that they had been close for many years. He wanted to please his lady as well as have a business talk with Ahmed. They went the next day.

'We were overjoyed to hear the news that you are both to become parents. Please accept our regrets for not having been in contact before today. I know that your market stalls were a great success at the gathering, which only shows the dedication and hard work you put into this. The other subject to discuss is our gold mines and what you want to do about them in the future.'

As this was about to become a discussion between the two men, Takamat went to make some mint tea.

'I am so happy about your plans to move to Abalessa and the proposed new city, but Ahmed will not hear of moving from here and I have to agree with him.. He was born here and all his family lives here. I must add that because of our new found wealth we have been able to spread it amongst all our relatives. They live in great splendour compared to what it was like before then. When our child is born, it will become a citizen of this city.' When they returned with the refreshments Marcus was still discussing the mines with Ahmed.

'Do you feel that they have been fully excavated, or is there still more to be found?' asked Marcus.

'That is impossible to know because the seams are still running in all directions and the miners are happy to be earning such a generous wage for their work. Takamat and I have retired because we have more gold than we will ever want. We have helped our family to have a high standard of living, and we have still much stored in secured places. Our child will be born into a rich family, but as we are both staying here I shall continue to manage the mine after you have moved on. You are still entitled to have an equal share which I shall have stored until you need it.' Tinan heard the tail end of this conversation and remarked.

'We also have gold stored here. When we leave we will need it to build our new city, but we will need guards to protect it during what could be a dangerous journey. If anything should happen as we travel north, we may need to replenish our treasury.'

The two men had agreed on the distribution of the gold, which was really only a formality as the four partners had riches beyond their perceptions. Ahmed had indicated that he would store all the future gold from the mines in a specially built stone warehouse. He would also deposit the details of the weight and the shared percentages with the assay office. During the following week the camels were loaded up with supplies. This entailed two hundred of the beasts. Not only was the gold to be transported but also food, water, clothing, tents and weapons and various household items such as a bath. As much as water was more precious than gold, Tinan hoped that she would use this in her new city.

Those who wanted to join the caravan were encouraged to do so, as this would give strength to their numbers should there be any trouble. Many of the clans were happy to follow their Queen. Marcus had spoken about the new kingdom which was to be built in the north and they were eager to see it for themselves.

Tinan had little regrets about leaving because she carried everything which she needed for the future in her head. As she had been a nomad for so long she had no ties to any one place therefore nostalgia was a sentiment which she had never known. The scholars and teachers were sad to see her leave and presented her with some beautiful gifts. Notable amongst these was a book with a highly decorated leather cover which was inlaid with precious jewels. Ruby, Cinnabar, Lapis Lazuli and Gold were beautifully worked into the leather. The pages had transparent golden butter paper between every two pages of text. These books contained much of what she had learnt, but the gift was made more precious because she knew that the knowledge given to her in this form was more important than gold.

When Tinan said farewell to these men, she gave them a purse of gold nuggets and told them that she would like them to continue to help scholars from all parts of the land, from all cultures and religions, and if women were suitably academic, to include them too. Saying goodbye to Takamat and Ahmed was sad for her, but she assured them that she would return one day when her work was completed. Marcus had convinced some of the men from his garrison that a journey to Abalessa would be very worthwhile for them. They would be given a choice of a new home or gold when they reached their destination, but some of his original legion would have followed him to the ends of the earth is he asked them: without any reward. They travelled for weeks without any incident, although occasionally they were visited by wandering Berbers who were curious about such a large group of camels and the numbers of people travelling with them.

As custom dictated, they were made welcome, shown hospitality and given food and drink. Marcus thought that it would be wise to spread the word that the Tuareg Queen was with them. This would have the intended impact of showing the strength of her entourage, and also to satisfy the curiosity of any raiders. He took the leader of the group of five men, and ushered him into her presence. When this man saw her sitting on a chair of ivory, encrusted with precious stones, he fell to his knees in wonder. He stared at her beautiful unveiled face, and her serene expression, but his eyes didn't miss a dozen men in robes and turbans standing behind her. They all had their faces covered, carried long spears and shields, some with tribal symbols which he recognised. He knew without doubt that he was in the presence of the Tuareg Queen and he never forgot it. Like all stories with impact, this one became exaggerated beyond proportion. The tale was repeated and grew with every repeating of it.

It was said the Queen Tinan travelled with an army of warriors, all resplendent in jeweled robes with weapons made of pure gold. The Queen was amazingly tall and beautiful (which was true), with magic eyes the colour of the Nile. She wore clothing woven from a cloth never before seen. This was adorned with precious stones of every hue and size. Although this was not entirely true, it had the desired effect to prohibit any unwelcome attack. When Marcus had first spoken to the clan's leaders, they understood that they had to show unity and form a phalanx around Tinan to indicate her strength and protection. This they were proud and happy to do.

As the caravan train neared the mountains, the peaks were just showing in the distance. It was agreed that they should camp the night some distance away and travel freshly in the morning to Abalessa. Marcus and Tinan were taking a walk, inspecting the camels when they became aware of a strange noise. The ground began to shake and little flying pieces of sand were peppering the ground. Marcus remembered this from the time when he had first found Tinan in the mountain cave, and he froze with the recollection. They couldn't hope to outrun the sand storm, but the tribal elders also recognised it and herded their families together inside the tents. The guards couldn't help the camels or the horses because there was no time, but Marcus told his men to tie all the camels together so that they could be easily found after the storm had passed. They knew how to cover their faces with turbans, turn their backs to the incoming wind, and if possible find something to cover their heads inside the tents. The storm would blow over, but the biggest problem was the sand. It could choke them and they would die if they didn't take steps to prevent inhaling the stuff. The tribesmen had seen this violent disturbance before and they knew how to fight it.

If it was a small storm they would be all right. If not, they would suffocate and be buried beneath the weight of the simoon. Some of the goats and sheep were pulled into the tent with them, and the small children were bundled up beneath any tightly woven cloth which would allow them to breathe without inhaling the particles. Marcus took Tinan into his arms, placed her silk shawl over both of their heads and then his large travelling cloak as well. The noise was horrendous as the walls of the tents shook and reverberated. At one stage someone's tent ripped and the sound of screams became the siren of doom. For Tinan this was a reminder of the terror and unbearable loss which she had suffered.

The difference was that today she had two strong arms holding her tight to comfort and protect her. After an hour or two the storm's fury had abated and the tent stopped shaking. Marcus told her that he was going to check the damage so he lifted the tent's peg where it had been fastened down. He was gone for a few minutes and then came back to her.

'It doesn't seem too bad my little one. All the tents are intact, but like ours they are covered with much sand, which has caused the sheer weight of the stuff to collapse them. This would account for the screams which would have seemed like the end for some of the poor people huddled beneath that violent assault.'

'Marcus I must go out and try to comfort these people who have followed me this far. I have led them into chaos and horror. Please come with me and help me to show strength and compassion to those in need.' As she stepped out from her tent, Tinan's hand flew to her mouth. They were completely surrounded by high sand dunes and there was no sign of the Ahaggar Mountain range.

Most of the tents had collapsed and some were half buried under the sand, but Tinan called to the strong younger men to come to her side, so that she could do a thorough search. As they began to crawl out, some were coughing, some had red eyes from the effects of this swirling genie, and others were still not able to move. She instructed each man to check every tent and report back to her if any were in dire need of assistance. There had been over five hundred souls who left Tombouctou with her, and of these only ten had perished. The rest had survived and were glad to be amongst the lucky ones.

Tinan ordered the surviving goats to be milked and the children to be given some fluids. After this, pregnant women and the elderly were given a little because there was hardly enough to do this, let alone a taste for everybody. Marcus called his guards, pleased to note that they had all survived. Then he instructed them to help with the tents and remove the sand which had fallen through and to release those which could be used again. All other items were to be gathered up and placed outside the tents for their owners to claim. When this was done, Tinan asked everyone who could move to form a group facing her as she had something to tell them. This was to be done by all who were able and healthy, excluding the elderly or heavily pregnant women. She stood on a little stool and removed the leather pouch from her waist band, holding the cylinder in her hand as she watched the fish's head quiver a little until it solidly pointed north. She spoke facing the entire assembly of her people.

'Today we have faced the worst terror that the desert can throw at us, but we have overcome this. We have no camels or horses, but we are going to walk into Abalessa tomorrow, starting at first light. I am taking you there with me. The journey will be long and hot so you cannot take anything with you to slow you down. I am leaving behind a division of guards who will stay here to care for the elderly, young children and the pregnant women who can't make this trip with us. After we arrive at Abalessa, I will send horses, camels and men to bring the others and all your belongings with them.'

Marcus was aware that the caravan's route towards the town of Abalessa had completely disappeared. They were in a predicament because the sand had covered up their exit and the mountain peaks were nowhere to be seen. There was no point of reference to be made, and with a large group travelling on foot, through the sand hills, it could be a very risky situation. Not only did Marcus have to consider the waiting survivors, but the now deceased camels had been carrying the much needed gold which had to be transported to the city. There were looks of dismay on many faces and some grumbling from those who couldn't see how they would possibly make that trek. A few of the discontented men approached Marcus with their fears. He told them.

'If Tinan has told you that she will take you safely to Abalessa, you must believe her. She has the power to do this. I suggest that you take this time to spend with your families, keeping them calm. Although we must leave some behind, you have my word that they will be reunited with you as soon as possible. Make sure that everyone has something to eat tonight even if it is just dried fruit. If this is not possible come and see me. I will organise some from my own store. Also tomorrow everyone must be well covered to protect themselves from the sun's rays. Even the women and children should wear turbans or shawls. That night the silence weighed heavily on these people.

To be separated from their loved ones was bad enough, but to leave and follow their Queen without clear direction seemed foolhardy. This was asking for total trust in her ability to lead them out of this predicament. Before he retired Marcus asked his men to wake him before the dawn's light as there was much to prepare before they moved out. He held Tinan in his arms, proud of the way that she had handled this catastrophe and knowing full well that she would overcome this and any future problems.

At daylight she went to her trunk, shook the sand from the white dress which she would wear into Abalessa and covered her head with a pale blue silk shawl and a golden band on which rested a small silver fan for her forehead. Her arms were covered with silver bracelets. When everyone had congregated outside their tents Marcus spoke to them.

'We are walking in triumph today with our Tuareg Queen. This is her home coming as well as our future.' Marcus took command of the march, instructing his guards to take up positions at either side of the ranks in case anyone needed help in keeping up. Tinan walked at the front holding her magic fish in her hand pointing the way, always following its head directing her to the north. The sand dunes had to be climbed and the hours seemed to drag on, but at last the peaks of the Ahaggar Mountains came into view.

'Ah, the mountains of Ahaggar are welcoming us, we are nearly there. Your Queen has delivered us from the desert safely. We will march into this city with our heads held high,' cried Marcus.

The news was greeted with shouts of appreciation which continued through the lines of all those gathered behind her. A few locals who had seen the distant sand storm couldn't believe their eyes. Here was a large group of people walking out of the desert. They were singing and waving their hands. Many people left their houses to witness this strange spectacle. When they saw Tinan, some thought that it was a mirage. How could anyone so serene and untouched by the simoon lead so many who looked weary and happy at the same time? As they entered the city someone asked a guard.

'Who are you and where are you from?'

'We are Queen Tinan Hinan's people and we have come from Tobouctou.' When this was repeated, a ripple of excitement ran through the bystanders and in unison they shouted.

'Hail Queen Tinan Hinan.' This chanting became louder as many left whatever they were doing and rushed to witness this incredible sight. Once all of the clans had entered and were given food and shelter by the townsfolk, Marcus borrowed some horses and made his way back over the same tracks to where the others had remained behind. This took many more hours to ferry them all to Abalessa, but Marcus then had to make a decision about the gruesome job of unloading the dead camels. He decided that it would be better to just cover them with sand to keep the vultures away, and return there after Tinan had been settled. He left a few trusted guards there and made sure that the location was visible by sticking flags into the surrounding area. Tinan was hailed as a Queen and greeted with awe as her fame spread far and wide. The clansmen told how she led them out of the sand dunes towards her chosen city. They believed that she had a godlike power which was accepted by all who loved and worshipped her. Within a day Marcus had organized a group of the strongest men to return to the camp on borrowed camels where they unearthed and transferred the goods which had been brought on this journey.

When she had rested, Tinan went about planning their marriage. It was to be a simple affair with all the clans and the local people invited. A large flat plain was chosen for the event, where all those who had tents were asked to erect them to form a circle. Those who did not were invited to join their fellow tribesmen. The scholars and other dignitaries were housed with Tinan and Marcus who had three large tents joined together. All invited guests from the surrounding areas brought their sheep and goats for the feast and the women made bread and other special food for the occasion. Tinan's ivory throne was placed outside the tent, with another special chair for Marcus. He wore the flowing robes which seemed to please her, and she wore the green silk dress which she had worn the night of their betrothal when they bound together their bodies and their souls. An elder from the tribe was chosen to conduct the ceremony, which he did by asking the couple to stand facing each other. He took their hands, placing his over hers, he asked her first.

'Is this man your husband?' She said. 'Yes, he is.' Then he turned to Marcus and asked.

'Is our Queen your wife?' He looked into her eyes and said. 'Yes.'

That was it. When these two faced the hundreds of happy faces the shouts of acceptance were heard resounding around the circle of tents. It was time for the festivities to start. Before the music and eating began in earnest, a Tuareg tribesman presented himself before the happy pair, bowing deeply. Marcus beckoned him to approach and waited for the man to speak.

'Tinan Hinan our wonderful Queen and your esteemed Consort, I speak on behalf of all who are gathered here today, in wishing you a long and happy life. You have brought us out of the desert to a land where we will make a new beginning under your guidance and wisdom. We consider our Queen to be the Mother of us all. We will always be your children and your servants.'

This speech was well received as the crowd in one voice repeated Queen Tinan Hinan over and over again. She raised her hand for silence, which fell immediately and spoke in a strong and clear voice.

'We have all been given a wonderful gift. That is when we conquered fear and chaos to become united here today. Not only to celebrate our wedding but to show that we are one people. There will be many opportunities for all to make a better life here and our strength will be found in helping each other. My tent will always be open to anyone who needs to talk to me. I strongly encourage that, because I am going to need your help as much as you will need mine.

Over the next few months we will be searching for a site to build my new city, and this will be an exciting chapter in our lives. Until then our tents will be our city. I suggest that you seek out the scholars who have travelled with us. They have great wisdom and will be my advisors. I will need their expertise and guidance for the future, but they can also help to explain what will be needed from us all to make that a reality. We both thank you for your kind wishes. We know that today is only the beginning of what will be an exciting lifetime for us all.'

This was greeted again with thunderous shouts of approval as Tinan sat down and smiled at Marcus. That night the air rang with music and laughter as the Tuaregs mixed with the local population and celebrated the marriage of their Queen. Tinan asked about the man who had given the speech of welcome, as she didn't know him. She was told that his name was Khaled, and that he had attended the games in Tombouctou.

His prowess with the bow and arrow was legendary. He was a man of high standing with his tribe. Marcus made a mental note to find out more about this man as there was something about Khaled which bothered him.

The feasting went on for many days. When night came Marcus and his new bride fell into bed close to exhaustion. She seemed weary which was understandable. He was content just to be by her side. When the wedding celebrations ended and the people had returned to their daily tasks, Marcus knew that the time was right to begin the mammoth operation of building a city. She had great ideas which she had formed some years ago, now she had the money to pay for it. Her fame had increased across the desert lands and even beyond, as builders, sculptors, designers, architects, and their slaves were enticed to be a part of something revolutionary and new.

She gave countless audiences and interviews. Marcus could see the strain begin to show, but she would hear none of it.

'This has to be done now. When it is finished I will rest and enjoy my work. Until then, please don't turn anyone away. Once the plans have been approved and the building commences, I will authorize others to oversee the production but until then I must continue. In the meantime, have you found the best site yet? This is very important Marcus because we will need a large volume of water to serve the houses as well as to irrigate the fields for food production.'

'I intend to ride out today with a few men to investigate a mountain stream which falls from a height as a waterfall into a natural large rocky reservoir. This could be suitable to channel the water, if we can enlarge the holding area and then direct it to our needs.' When he returned Marcus was very confident that the water held in the mountains would be a good start. There was more than one stream which cascaded over the rocks into a river, and with some labour, this could be gathered and diverted. Although this was a very mountainous region, there were plenty of palms and plants which spoke well of the soil's ability to produce crops. The height of the mountains made excellent vantage points in case of any threatening danger from marauders. Tinan decided that her city would be built amongst these mountains, but Marcus was appalled.

'It will take years to build anything at that height. Just getting men and materials up there would be enough to cause all sorts of problems, but your people are not mountain dwellers and I can't see them wanting to live anywhere unless they have the firm ground beneath their feet.'

'They will be doing just that. The Orient which produced some of my beautiful silk robes has other skills to offer. I have been talking through an interpreter to a man who assures me that there is such a method used to build at great heights. In his homeland they use something called bamboo to construct wooden bridges from one side to the other of such high structures. We would have to use local timbers as an alternative where the workers can walk from one side to the other, across the constructions carrying their tools or anything else needed. They are quite safe, as these bridges have another rail behind the builders to stop them falling. These places built up high would not be for everyone, so I have also had meetings with other artisans who can create small houses in the caves for those who prefer to be closer to the ground.'

'I should have known that you would find a way to build your skyscraper city and try to accommodate everyone's needs. We still have plenty of gold in reserve, but in a year's time we may need to make a journey back to Tombouctou to replenish this.'

The buildings and construction now began in earnest as many people came from the town just to watch this marvelous transformation. The shallow sections between the hills were filled with buildings of three and four levels, but they were so designed that they abutted against the rocks which held them fast. The caves that had been cut by nature were now widened into whole rooms and joined by small hallways cut and chipped through the rock. Slaves were used as they were plentiful. They were well fed and looked after on Tinan's orders, so they worked happily on all the building sites. Their lives were far more comfortable than working in the salt mines, and they appreciated the difference.

As the city began to rise Tinan took a break, suggesting to Marcus that they could leave the project in the hands of their managers and perhaps make the journey to Tombouctou. He was agreeable to this, arranging for one hundred camels to make this journey south and carry the gold back to Abalessa from Tombouctou. Many guards were also needed to protect this caravan which took off in fair weather. Tinan wore her magic fish attached to a belt around her waist, just in case of trouble. Marcus had organized his men to wear the dress of the Tuareg with blue turbans wrapped around their faces.

He didn't notice that Khaled was amongst this group. All went well without any incident until they were just a day away from their destination. Marcus ordered a rest at the oasis to fill their water containers before moving on. How did it happen? Somehow his container went missing. He was offered another from one of the men travelling with them. This man was Khaled. All the men had covered faces so Marcus never knew that Khaled had put poison in it. When he took a drink in the heat of the day Marcus toppled from his horse to the ground. This caused a terrible scene, because nobody suspected that there had been any foul play. Tinan rushed to his side, put his head in her lap and screamed as his eyes turned back into his head without a word escaping from his lips. Because they were so close to the city, she instructed them to make haste in case anything could be done to help her husband. They were made welcome as a caravan of this size always attracted attention and this was no exception. When Tinan was recognised she was hailed as a visiting Queen.

She quickly called for medical help but when they took Marcus's body to a mortuary, she knew that he was dead. There were no suspicions about his death, because Khaled used a powerful but untraceable poison. Many had died in the desert without any obvious causes. The bad news spread quickly. Takamat hurried to meet her at the apartment which had been presented to Tinan for her stay. Both women embraced as old friends, and although Takamat had heard the news about the death of Marcus, she was more amazed when she observed that Tinan showed little grief.

'My dear friend Takamat, it seems that everyone that I love dies before my eyes. I truly loved this man, but his life was not mine to share. I have lost everything that I hold dear except you my loving and faithful friend. I have no more tears to shed. His funeral will be held here before I return to Abalessa.'

Takamat began to cry for her dearest friend and all the sorrow which had plagued her life. Fate was unkind to someone who ill deserved it.

'You must come and stay with us. We have a large house and plenty of rooms fit for a Queen. Ahmed and I have a daughter who is two years old and we would be honoured to have you spend your time here.'

Accepting this kindness, Tinan did move into their home and found some solace from the devastating loss of her husband. Ahmed and Takamat looked after her with care and concern, but when the cremation was over Tinan thanked them and told her friends that she had to return to Abalessa. She informed Ahmed that the large group of camels was there to transport the gold back to Abalessa. Although she felt little joy in this without Marcus, she knew that her people needed more gold for the completion of their city. Tinan said goodbye to her friends and their little daughter. She also took more camels, horses and slaves who were needed for the ongoing development of her city.

There was shock and disbelief from the entire city when she arrived back with the news of her husband's death.

Apart from dressing in black and covering her face for a mourning period of thirty days, it was then back to work She had promised her people to build them a city and she would not let them down. When her palace was completed she moved into it without any fanfare. Her days were still filled with decisions: choices of colours for the interior, fabrics for the cushions and curtains, objects of fine crafted silverware and so on. At night she was restless and was seen to pace up and down the marble halls alone and lost. The staff and courtiers loved her as their Queen but also as a woman. They fiercely guarded her privacy as well as obeyed her every command.

Just before the mourning period had ended, Tinan made a discovery which she least expected. She was pregnant. Although she was amazed at this revelation, she didn't want to make any announcements until it was too obvious for her to keep hidden. Debra, her chief lady-in-waiting became Tinan's confidante and strength. Debra wouldn't allow anyone to see Tinan unless it was first discussed with her, and even then the time was strictly monitored.

She became the Queen's messenger, informing the builders and artisans that the Queen was still in mourning and indisposed. If there were any pressing problems, Debra handled them. The work continued and now the city's skyline rose in high peaks. The architects had also suggested that mud would be a good way to quickly erect buildings for the commercial use in the market square and other meeting places for the larger population. This was to be done in a similar way to the mud buildings in Tombouctou and included cafes and other places of social activities. The people of Abalessa now enjoyed their city and became proud of its beautiful streets and gardens.

The important use of agriculture had been earlier designed by Tinan with some help from her advisors. It worked perfectly.

The fields which were planted with crops were watered by a drip feed system from the mountain streams. Channels were cut into ditches alongside the seeded beds which enabled the farmers to spread the water to reach them. This way the amount of water was controlled and the plants flourished. Now the population had food to sell and the economy of this city took shape too. Everything seemed to be going to plan for Tinan, including the growth of the child inside her. She told Debra that she would be inspecting the latest additions to the city.

'Please have my carriage ready tomorrow. I will be taking a little journey to the outskirts to see the progress of the city. I will need a canopy over my head for protection from the sun, as well as six of my guards to accompany me.'

The beautiful additions to the high mountain dwellings as well as the sculpted caves at ground level were pleasing to her. For a moment she wished that Marcus could see this wonderful city spread out and flourishing. When she returned to the Palace, Khaled was waiting to help her alight from her carriage. He noticed with surprise that she was with child. This news had not been forthcoming from the others who worked for the Queen. As much as Khaled had never accepted Marcus as the Queen's consort, a child would be another Tuareg to continue the royal line. He was determined that nothing should prevent this from happening. He called a special meeting with the other leaders and told them that the Queen was with child. Every precaution must be taken to ensure the safe arrival of that child and continuation of the Tuareg dynasty. This was highly unnecessary because Tinan could do no wrong in their eyes and they would die for her if need be.

Within two months Tinan gave birth to a daughter, naming her Kella. It was a natural birth with Debra on hand to help.

The child was the image of her mother with the same blue eyes which had captivated her father, Marcus. This was a reason for more rejoicing. After one week, Tinan acknowledged the crowd's euphoria from her balcony. She became totally absorbed in the daily life of her daughter, so she called her senior advisor to announce that she was putting any further construction into his hands. He was honoured but told her.

'Your Majesty, I appreciate this mark of your respect, but my work here is nearly finished. Before the year's end I shall return to Tombouctou. I have given much tuition to those men younger and smarter than myself. Hopefully this tradition will continue in your wonderful city.'

Tinan was sorry to hear this but she knew that he deserved to spend his retirement in the place of his birth. This somehow reminded her of a conversation which she had some years ago with Takamat. A thought came into her head as she spoke to this man standing before her.

'You go with my blessings and appreciation for the wonderful work which you have done. There is a small favour I would ask of you when you return home. It is this: My friends Ahmed and Takamat Khaldun live in Tombouctou. They are a well known family and should be easy to find. She has been like a sister to me. I would like you to invite her and her family to come to Abalessa for a visit.'

Her advisor was only too happy to do this. Within six months Tinan was informed that a small caravan was headed along the trade route to Abalessa. She was overjoyed. This had to be Takamat, Ahmed and their daughter. When the caravan arrived, only three passengers dismounted but Ahmed was not one of them. Takamat could see that Tinan was expecting her husband to be there too but she waited until they were inside Tinan's private rooms before she spoke about the reason for this.

'It happened not long after our second daughter Fatima, was born. Ahmed had gone to the mine to check out a small problem which had been reported by one of his men. There was a cave in and he was buried alive. When they finally excavated the mine's contents, his poor body was broken into pieces, and he was beyond help.'

'Oh Takamat this is so hard to accept. You were perfectly happy with a lovely family. It seems unbelievable that we are both alone with just our children. You must bring your girls to meet Kella, who is still a baby and trying to sit up. She will be so happy to see them.'

Takamat and her two daughters stayed for nearly a year.

The city of Abalessa captivated them and she marvelled at the wonderful buildings, houses, gardens and fields sown with abundant crops. Her two daughters had the run of the palace and accumulated friends everywhere. Tinan felt that she had the right to question her friend about her future.

'I am planning to make one last trip to Tombouctou because Marcus had left some hidden gold reserves there which would be safer stored here in the mountains of Abalessa. What does the future hold for you now? Do you intend returning to Tombouctou or would you prefer to remain here?'

Takamat knew that this conversation would eventually take place so she was pleased that Tinan had raised it first.

'It certainly would be a suitable plan to travel in a large escorted caravan with you and return home. The gold mines are still in production, and I need to check their progress. As far as the future is concerned, my daughters love living here with Kella and yourself, and it would be difficult for them to settle down at home after living in a Palace but that is not the only reason. I didn't want to burden you with anymore sadness, but when I left to make this journey I heard whispers that Marcus had been poisoned. I now fear for your life too.'

Tinan's face blanched as she had never thought that her husband had died from anything other than natural causes. Although still a fairly young man, it was not uncommon for men to die at his age.

'If what you say is correct, I feel ashamed and saddened that someone from this city would do that, but I do not fear for my own life. I have many guards and courtiers who are loyal to me, but after hearing this, I shall meet with the men who served under Marcus and arrange for a closer bodyguard at all times. We will make that journey together and bring back as much as our camels can carry. I have the perfect place in mind to store our gold when we return with it. As to your choice to live here with your daughters, I welcome it with all my heart. We have shared so much in our lives, but from now on we will work towards the enrichment of our children's lives and the greater good for the people of Abalessa.'

Takamat had her own apartments within the palace where she lived with her two daughters, Tiski and Fatima. They attended classes with Kella when she was old enough to do so, where the three girls became as inseparable as sisters. When a year had passed Tinan changed her mind about taking the journey, but she encouraged Takamat to travel to Tombouctou, in her place.

'I will give you a letter with my Royal Seal and instructions as to where our gold reserves are located, permission to transport them here and a large escort for this purpose. This must be kept completely secret until you are ready to leave on your journey back to Abalessa. I will explain my intention to only two of Marcus's trusted guards. Aurelio and Francesco will pack the gold into sacks of salt before they are loaded onto the camels. This should safeguard their passage home.'

This was completely understood by Takamat. If she and her daughters were going to live in Abalessa, it was only right that she should do something to help Tinan. She felt happy that she could leave her children in the care of Debra and her staff. The journey south was made without any problems because the two guards Aurelio and Francesco were alert and aware of this important expedition. The sacks of gold were treated in the way that Tinan requested. Hidden in bags of salt they were loaded and transported on and off the camels without any fuss, eventually arriving safely back at Abalessa. The bags were taken to her private chambers under cover of darkness, where Tinan had to arrange their transportation to the final place she had in mind. There were no such strongholds in the palace to store this precious metal so it had to be done secretly and soon. Aurelio was summoned to the Queen's private chambers where she conveyed her orders for the gold to be stored in a certain cave.

'Unfortunately this will be a slow and arduous process because both you and Franceso will have to do this alone. I will have the sacks brought around to the back of the palace with instruction that the 'salt' is to be ready for transport to our storage depots. They will be loaded by my palace guards onto a horse-drawn dray: a total of one hundred bags. That part will be done for you, but you will have to unload them yourselves.'

'Yes of course Your Majesty, we loaded them in Tombouctou and we will certainly be able to unload them into the cave.'

'Excellent!' said Tinan. 'Tonight I will follow you on horseback and direct you to the cave. The moonlight should make our task a little easier. One more thing, please bring the two shovels with the sacks when you leave here.'

There was still a major concern for Tinan. That was the courtier Khaled. Although she was never to know that he had been responsible for the death of Marcus, intuitively Tinan always felt that this man was dangerous and not to be trusted, so she enlisted the help of Debra.

'Tonight I have to make a pilgrimage to a place where I have to be completely alone to mourn the death of two members of my family who died here many years ago. Knowing I am watched by a certain man who would think nothing of following and intruding on my privacy, I want you to make sure that he is occupied for the night. His name is Khaled. I am sure that you know him by sight.'

'Yes I do know him. I have seen him skulking around the Palace. He is not popular with the guards as he is always plotting against someone or constantly complaining about things which are none of his business. What exactly do you want me to do?'

'I know that he often spends time in the palace kitchens sipping wine with the staff. I want you to slip something into his drink. This will only put him into a heavy sleep, but you must be sure that he gets it. Do you think that you will be able to do this?'

'Yes, my Lady. I would do anything that you ask of me. I will go to the kitchen on some pretext and wait for him to arrive. He will not be suspicious of me. When he has had one glass of wine, I will offer him another with the sleeping draught in it. When he nods off, I will enlist the help of a trusted man to take him and leave him outside the city somewhere.'

'That sounds like a good idea, but if by some chance he does not visit the kitchen and you cannot manage to do this, you must inform me immediately. Whatever happens please come to my chambers and tell me when this has been successfully achieved.'

Whilst the construction of the mountain city was being erected, Tinan had told the master builders to excavate a certain cave which would be used to store weapons in case of a siege or attack from other sources, so it was already prepared to receive the 'salt sacks' now. What was also put into place was a useful strategy to contain the 'weapons' in such a manner as to be hidden from prying eyes. When the cave was excavated and a large pit had been dug at the back, the entrance of the cave was filled with many large boulders through which only a child could crawl. That was how it appeared to any onlookers, but

Tinan's senior advisor had devised a plan for access before he returned to Tombouctou. This was in the form of a maze, which could only be traversed with the knowledge of when to turn left or right. Otherwise if this route was not taken exactly, a person could get hopelessly lost and never find their way out of this labyrinth.

Tinan knew that this would not be an easy task for the two men, but she had earlier visited the cave, placing little white chalk marks on the narrow passage way needed to follow. There was just enough room for them to carry two bags each at a time and to see in the moonlight to follow the signs.

This was accomplished without any problems. The two men had unloaded and packed the pit at the back of the cave with ninety nine large sacks of salt and gold which was then covered over with sand. Before they left Tinan rewarded them with a small sack of gold nuggets each with strict instructions that they were to use it very carefully. She had to trust that this would be the case. She returned to the cave, standing there for a few minutes, reliving all its terrible memories. Silently she said a prayer for Habib and her stillborn child. Then she erased all signs of the chalk marks which led to her treasure.

After a few months she told Takamat about the cave's contents as well as the secret passage through a maze to where the gold was stored.

'It is not likely that we will need these riches, and I would prefer them to stay hidden forever in this place , but if you think that you will ever need to go there, I am going to have the details recorded on the two silver bracelets which we always wear. It will not mean anything to anyone else except you and me, but if perhaps one day you want to tell your children, you will need to understand the directions.'

'But won't that alert anyone else to the location?'

'No, they would have to be shown which cave that these instructions refer to, and there are hundreds of caves in our region.

The two bracelets will only show a series of 'left or right.' The letters will be engraved in two languages which are Egyptian Hieroglyphics and the Ethiopic Ge'ez Syllable script in a sequence which would be in a circle with no end or beginning. It would not be possible to apply the letters unless you knew where they began. As you know the symbol for "L" is a lion lying down and the symbol for "R" is a grain of rice in the Egyptian letters, but the Ethiopian symbols are just funny decorative scribbles and therefore impossible to understand unless you are aware of their purpose.

'Where would this sequence begin? If they are in a constant circle, how could anyone know where to begin?'

'That is easy. Each bracelet is secured by a ring which fits over a post. This post is attached to one side of the circle. To close the bracelet the ring has to latch over the post. So you have one unmovable post and one movable ring. After the bracelet has been opened, begin at the beginning where the post is attached, reading from left to right until you reach the ring at the end.

It doesn't matter if the bracelet is one way or the other, as long as you follow the symbols in sequence from the post first and not the ring. That is how the location is to be followed. My silversmith will engrave the directions of left or right without knowing what they represent. Using Egyptian pictures and Ethiopian symbols as letters, it would be impossible to decipher this code. As you know the skyline of Abalessa is in the design, but these engraved marks will be seen there without ever relating to any visible part of that skyline.'

'This all seems a little complicated, but it will be as you wish. Please show me the location of this cave and then I can forget about it unless something happens to change our lives.'

They visited the cave's location without actually entering it, but Takamat felt sure that she could find it again. The boulders at the entrance completely covered it, so Tinan showed her a tiny natural indentation on one of them which could be easily recognised to identify this particular cave.

Takamat and Debra were a good team and ran the Royal household leaving Tinan to continue her other duties. Although Tinan and Takamat shared many private moments, Tinan had a bodyguard within call at all times. There were some whispers that Takamat sometimes stayed too long within Tinan's private rooms. Debra was not impressed with gossip, so she called a meeting to dispel these rumours. She knew the legend about Tinan's life before she became their Queen and she knew that Takamat had saved the Queen's life on at least two occasions. She had helped to deliver Tinan's stillborn baby when they were both much younger. These two women were tribal sisters. Debra did not find anything unusual about their relationship.

This was not Khaled's opinion when he heard the same rumours. If the Queen and Takamat were lovers this would mean big trouble.

Whatever the intimacy between the two women, it was not suitable for this kingdom to exist with these dangerous innuendoes. He summoned the bodyguard and asked his opinion about the circulating rumours which had come to his notice. The guard didn't like this man and he knew that Marcus quietly voiced the same opinion, but Aurelio had to be careful as he knew that Khaled held some sway here, and also had some powerful friends.

'No Sir, my lady needs this time private time with her friend. The duties of a Queen are taxing and if they spend time together, it because the Queen wishes it so. They both have lovely voices as I have heard them singing in a foreign language together, and if this makes the Queen happy it is her right.'

Khaled was not satisfied. He decided to find out for himself, so he found a place well hidden in the garden outside her bedchamber, where he could see and hear what was happening. He saw Tinan open the door to Takamat and watched as she led her outside to the balcony.

Both women wore filmy nightdresses with little underclothing. Khaled was aware of the outline of their firm bodies in the moonlight. After a few words and some soft laughing a brush was handed to Takamat, who proceeded to brush Tinan's hair. When she finished doing this she asked if she should braid her hair with beads or silver jewelry. Tinan declined but handed her a flute, whilst she picked up a lovely harp. They sat closely together, singing and swaying in rhythm to the well remembered songs of long ago. The moon went behind some clouds, settling the night with a feeling of peace and appreciation of the harmony sung by these two lovely women. After a short time Takamat rose, embraced Tinan and said goodnight. Watching this, Khaled was still not convinced. How can two women flaunt themselves, behave in such a licentious manner without there being something more to their behaviour? He knew that Tinan's hold on her people was a strong one which he fully supported for the good of the Tuareg. Somehow he had to remove that other woman in a way that wouldn't point any suspicion at him.

The Court Council had decreed that since Tinan had no male heir, the descent would be through the female, so her daughter had to be protected until she was of the age to wed and continue the royal line.

That was not how Khaled felt about her Mother. Knowing that the two women went for regular walks close to the outskirts of the city, he decided to take a risk. Tinan decided to visit the spot where their cave was located with Takamat just to assure herself that Takamat knew exactly where it was. Before she could do this, Takamat noticed some pretty little flowers growing in a crevice near the boulders and bent to pick them.

She heard him first, a soft growl and then a roar. She stumbled on the stony ground but the large cat seemed to focus on Tinan. The guard realized what was happening and drew his sword, but the cheetah's eyes were locked onto Tinan. It began to run at her with a blurring speed. Takamat used all her strength to throw herself in the cheetah's path. He killed her before the guard's sword found him.

Tinan fainted. When her bodyguard called out to the men who were tending the horses, they came running quickly. It was too late. Tinan never came to terms with the loss of her friend but showed very little external emotion. Takamat was given a special funeral. Tinan knew that she had died saving her life, but she also knew that she could never feel close to anyone ever again. The heavens had decreed this. Her losses had numbed her heart. From that day forward, Tinan had very little to do with her own daughter.

Debra was asked to raise her. She also instructed her court that when her time came she was to be buried next to Takamat's grave. Tinan kept the small bracelet which she had made for her friend and insisted that on her death, it was to be buried with her. When this event happened in Abalesssa, Tinan was mourned by thousands of Tuaregs and Bedouins alike. Her burial chamber was kept secret for centuries as a mark of respect for the 'Mother of us All.'

Before she died, Tinan made sure that her daughter and Takamat's two girls knew everything which had happened in her life. This story was to be handed down from daughter to daughter so that one day the secret of the two silver bracelets found with Tinan's body might be revealed.

A.E. Stewart

This author began telling stories at the age of six in a Sydney boarding school. Once lights were out, tall tales were in. 'Ghost stories' were the most popular but it was the repetition of speaking and composing which produced words at a speed far quicker than anyone could write them down that started the treadmill. Such a place became the nursery where a vivid imagination was born.

A.E. lived in England for some time prior to the Queen's Coronation, where a wealth of experience with the 'Cockney' way of life and the different accents of the London population was gained.

The series of 'The Silver Thieves' was born from a younger brother's inspiration. His love of Silver and the borrowed 'Sterling Silver and their Hallmarks' book became the catalyst for this writer's literary intentions.

If you enjoyed this book, please leave a review on Amazon.

Contact A.E. ....jacana3@bigpond.com

The Queen's Coronation Spoon is stolen, leaving Myra to avert a national disaster.

Then in 1952 she comes into possession of a spoon stolen right from under the nose of Captain Cook himself, straight off the Endeavour in 1770.

Shrewd buyers circle, but a stubborn Myra obsessed with discovering the origin of Cook's spoon, hangs on through insurmountable challenges.

Excitement turns to disaster for Myra during the Queen's Coronation but the discovery of a cache of silver lifts her spirits; until religious fanatics ruin her honeymoon in Timbuktu.

A race against time to save the crumbling manuscripts of Timbuktu demand John's serious attention, but Myra's needs take priority as her life hangs in the balance.

The translation of the origin and the engraved message of the silver bracelets are revealed to John, but has he heard the whole story?

TINAN HINAN

A. E. STEWART

In the fourth century A.D. a young woman unites the nomadic Tuareg tribes of the Saharan Desert region.

Loved and known as the "Mother of us all," she is called Queen Tinan Hinan.

She commissions two silver bracelets, the engravings forming a map to the hiding place of a vast treasure.

But this connection to an ancient culture prevents anyone from unlocking the secret.